Dear Reader,

You're about to experience a revolution in reading—BookShots.

BookShots are a whole new kind of book—100 percent story-driven, no fluff, always under $5.

I've written or co-written nearly all the BookShots and they're among my best novels of any length.

At 150 pages or fewer, BookShots can be read in a night, on a commute, or even on your cell phone during breaks at work.

I hope you enjoy *Private: Gold.*

All my best,

James Patterson

P.S.

For special offers and the full list of BookShots titles, please go to **BookShots.com**

BOOK**SHOTS**

PRIVATE: GOLD

JAMES PATTERSON
with JASSY MACKENZIE

BOOKSHOTS

Little, Brown and Company

New York Boston London

Copyright © 2017 by James Patterson

BookShots / Little, Brown and Company
Hachette Book Group
1290 Avenue of the Americas, New York, NY 10104
bookshots.com

First Edition: May 2017

BookShots is an imprint of Little, Brown and Company, a division of Hachette Book Group, Inc. The Little, Brown name and logo are trademarks of Hachette Book Group, Inc. The BookShots name and logo are trademarks of JBP Business, LLC.

The Hachette Speakers Bureau provides a wide range of authors for speaking events. To find out more, go to hachettespeakersbureau.com or call (866) 376-6591.

ISBN 978-0-316-43871-1
LCCN 2016962915

10 9 8 7 6 5 4 3 2 1

LSC-C

Printed in the United States of America

PRIVATE: GOLD

PROLOGUE

ALONE IN HIS office, Khosi Khumalo waited for the visitor who was his last hope. He was nervous about this meeting, more so because the man was late. He glanced through the window. The latch had been damaged in the recent burglary and he'd fixed it with a piece of twisted wire. Outside, the sky was darkening and the hum of traffic was starting to subside. But he'd willingly stay here till midnight or beyond if this visitor could deliver what he'd promised…information.

Khosi was desperate for the vital link that would allow him to pull together everything he'd learned over the past few weeks. They knew he was digging, and they were trying to stop him. The recent break-in was proof of that, he was sure. He'd hidden two sets of backup data in different places, and although they'd found one, they had missed the other.

But he didn't know who "they" were—not yet.

He hoped that by the time he left tonight, things would be different. Then he could share the knowledge with his business partner. It would turn everything around, and give the two of them a fighting chance again. He hadn't wanted to burden Joey with what he'd learned, not when Joey was preoccupied with the day-to-day survival of Private Johannesburg, their fledgling investigation business.

The shrill ring of the doorbell made him jump. Instinctively he glanced at the empty space where the video surveillance screen had been. It had been stolen, of course, together with everything else of value.

Khosi checked that his pistol was holstered on his belt. Then he hurried to the lobby and opened the door. "Mr. Steyn?"

The man who shuffled in looked as furtive and dispirited as he had sounded when he'd called earlier. They'd taken everything from him, he'd said, and it certainly appeared true. Dressed in shabby jeans and a threadbare shirt that hung on his lean frame, he seemed much further down on his luck than Khosi was. He carried piles of files and documents in a makeshift wooden crate with nails jutting from it. In a soft voice, he greeted Khosi.

"Let me help you with that," Khosi offered, taking one side of the crate, but Steyn nearly dropped his side, and the flimsy container started to fall apart. Khosi made a grab for the documents as they slid to the floor. Wooden slats clattered around him, and something sharp jabbed him painfully in the thigh.

"Hey! Careful, there," he warned as he picked up a dog-eared folder. Behind him he heard Steyn mumble, "Sorry."

A minute later, and Khosi had retrieved the fallen papers and pressed the nails back into place. His thigh was stinging…the crate looked old and dirty and he made a mental note to get a tetanus booster as soon as possible.

He placed the crate on the desk, feeling surprisingly tired after the short walk. Well, it was only Tuesday, but the week had already been filled with stress. He sat down, realizing that the room was starting to swim around him. Desperately, he tried to gather his thoughts.

"Tell me who they are," he began, but he slurred the words. Deep inside him, a flame of panic blazed. He slumped onto the desk, aware of Steyn pulling on a pair of latex gloves before approaching him. Steyn's movements were no longer downtrodden and shuffling, but fast and purposeful.

"No!" he wanted to shout, but the words would not come; a darkness was rushing up to meet him. He tried to channel his panic into action but the flame flickered and died. With a jerk, his pistol was snatched from the holster.

He felt his hand being lifted; gloved fingers forced the gun into his own grasp. Khosi had time only for a pang of terrible regret that his own desperation had driven him so trustingly into this trap.

Cold steel, hard against his temple.

Then…nothing.

CHAPTER 1

THE CLEAN-UP crew had missed a bloodstain. Joey Montague saw it as soon as he lifted the steel filing cabinet. Now dried to a deep rust color, the blood had seeped through a crack in the floorboards, darkening the wood around it.

It was ingrained now, a permanent reminder of the disasters that the past two weeks had brought. Their last contracts canceled, a devastating burglary, and finally his business partner's suicide. On Wednesday morning, he'd walked in to find Khosi Khumalo's body slumped on the floor with a fatal bullet wound in his temple. In death, Khosi had looked peaceful, and his service pistol was lying near his right hand.

Then, as now, Joey's first reaction had been an anguished, "Why?"

But that question could never be answered. Khosi hadn't even left a note.

The new tenants could worry about removing the floor stain. Joey was vacating the building. After Khosi's death, he'd been tempted to close up shop for good, abandon his hopes and dreams and go back to the corporate world. But in the end, his fighting spirit prevailed and he'd decided simply to scale down. He would run Private Johannesburg from his home office until he was back on his feet—emotionally and financially. He would carry on trying to make a success of Khosi's legacy, even in these difficult circumstances.

He still remembered the call, seven months ago, that had lured him out of his pressurized office job and catapulted him into a different and riskier world.

"Joey? It's me, Khosi! Listen, bro, I've got a great opportunity here. You know I've been running my own show as a PI the past few years? Well, on my last case, I ended up working with an international firm called Private. Long story short, Jack Morgan, the owner, proposed that I open a branch here. Private Johannesburg. Bro, this is going to be huge—the potential is unlimited, but I need help. I need a business partner in this venture. I could use your expertise in financial forensics. You want to come discuss it over a whiskey after work?"

He'd signed the deal with Khosi that night and resigned from his corporate job the next day, confident he was making the right decision. Now, he was no longer sure.

A gust of wind rattled the wire-fastened window latch, distracting Joey from his thoughts. He didn't have time to stare at the floor; he needed to get the last of the furniture in the truck because a summer storm was approaching fast. Dark thunderheads were swallowing Johannesburg's skyline. The sight of those high-rise buildings, clad in pale concrete and glimmering glass, had become familiar to him. They were a symbol of hope that one day he could move the business out of this humble suburb where rentals were cheap but crime was escalating, and into the CBD. Now, the storm had turned the skyscrapers to a dull, forbidding gray. The trees in the nearby park swayed wildly in the gale, and litter scudded down the sidewalk.

As the first drops of rain spattered the dusty glass, Joey's cell phone started ringing.

"Montague," he answered, leaning his elbows on the cold steel cabinet.

"Is that Private Johannesburg? It's Isobel Collins speaking. I'm looking to hire a bodyguard urgently." The caller sounded breathless and Joey picked up an American accent.

You're a couple of days too late for that, Miss Collins, Joey thought sadly, as lightning split the sky. He was going to tell her that Khosi, the firm's only qualified bodyguard, had tragically died, but she spoke again.

"Please, I need your help."

Joey caught sight of his own reflection in the darkening glass. Short-cropped black hair, deep-set hazel eyes, hard jaw. His expression was grim, making him look older than his age of thirty-five. Khosi had always joked that Joey lost ten years every time he smiled.

He moved away from the window, where rain was drumming the panes.

"There's nobody who can help," he explained in heavy tones.

"It's urgent." Had she heard him? Perhaps the storm was affecting the signal; her voice crackled down the line.

"What's the problem?" he asked.

"I've just arrived in Johannesburg from JFK. I need a bodyguard for the weekend. I booked someone before I left, but he didn't meet me at the airport."

"I'm sorry. No guards are available." As he spoke, thunder crashed overhead.

"What was that? I didn't hear you. This connection is terrible."

"I said we don't have a qualified guard at this time." He shouted the words, but they were obliterated by the clatter of hail on the roof.

Clearly, the elements were conspiring against him.

"You're on the top of my list," Isobel replied. "Private, I mean. I have other options, but you're my first choice. So if you could…I'd really appreciate it."

Joey was about to repeat his refusal, but he hesitated. There was something in her voice that was making him uneasy.

"Please, I'm short of time," she added, and Joey heard a tone in her voice he recognized all too well.

Isobel Collins was badly scared.

Perhaps she was frightened of traveling alone in a country with such a high crime rate. Most visitors were paranoid about safety in South Africa, even though there were always the few who tried to climb out of their safari vehicles to hand-feed the lions.

Suddenly Joey thought: why shouldn't he take the job himself? Although he didn't have practical experience in the field, he'd completed a close-protection course and a self-defense seminar during his first month with Private. Shepherding a tourist around the city would be an easy job, and it would fill the empty weekend ahead that he'd been dreading.

"I'll do it," he promised.

"Thank you," Isobel replied, in a voice filled with relief. "I really appreciate it—it's my first time here, and I feel out of my depth. The city's different than I thought it would be…Way bigger, for one thing. And busier."

"Are you still at the airport?"

"No, I've left already. I'm driving to my lodgings."

"Give me the address and I'll meet you there." He assumed she'd be heading to the Central Business District, where most tourists stayed—although travelers usually came for business, rather than leisure.

Founded in the 1880s as a gold-rush city, Johannesburg had always attracted people looking to make fast money. Today the thriving CBD, in the suburb of Sandton, was filled with an aggressive, contagious energy. Beyond it, in every direction, the city grew and sprawled.

Although Joey found Johannesburg's history and culture fascinating, he had to acknowledge that for the majority of tourists, the place was merely a stop-off point for the more scenic towns and game reserves nearby. But even so, it was where the wealthy people of South Africa lived. It was the country's business hub, where the money flowed and deals were done.

The Sandton CBD was accessible by high-speed train from the airport, and he wished he'd had a chance to tell Isobel, because it was far easier to take the train than fight through Johannesburg's notoriously congested roads.

But, as it happened, Joey had guessed her destination completely wrong.

"I'm staying in Kya Langa," she said.

"You're staying *where?*" He hadn't misheard, but he was hoping she'd gotten the place name wrong.

"Number three Foundry Road, Kya Langa. It's in eastern Johannesburg."

"Yes, I know where it is, I used to do work in the area, but…"

Adrenaline flooded through him. Miss Collins was on her way to one of the most dangerous places in the city, where slum housing had sprung up around an abandoned metalworks factory, causing the lower-income neighborhood to decline drastically. That was just one of the reasons why crime in that part of Johannesburg had spiraled out of control. There were others, even more serious.

Why was she heading there? He wished he knew, but he supposed that as a bodyguard, it wasn't his place to ask. In any case, questions would only waste valuable time.

"I'll get to you as fast as I can," he promised.

CHAPTER 2

NO TIME TO lose...Isobel Collins would be in danger from the minute she left the highway. Hurriedly, Joey lifted the filing cabinet into the truck. It was empty; it had been broken into and ransacked during the burglary.

There was only one more piece to move—Khosi's desk—but it was the heaviest item of all. Joey remembered joking with Khosi when they moved in, as the two of them had struggled with the solid mahogany table, that it weighed more than any piece of furniture had a right to do. Khosi had laughed, and said it was a lucky desk; the man at the second-hand shop had told him so.

Khosi had always been that way. Joking, lighthearted, optimistic. Grasping one side of the table while the removal-truck driver took the other, Joey was struck again by the tragedy of his business partner's suicide.

Private Johannesburg had signed contracts for a major, and potentially very lucrative, investigation into the problem of illegal mining in eastern Johannesburg. He and

Khosi had put together a full-service solution for the mines. In addition to the investigation side, they had provided round-the-clock private security services to guard various entrances. They'd made a huge investment in the project, hiring the highest caliber of guards they could source. With the deals signed, they'd believed the funds were well spent and that nothing could go wrong. But a change in government policy had killed the project, and wiped out the investment they'd made.

In the weeks after the deals were canceled, Khosi had been out of the office for long stretches. He hadn't told Joey the details of what he was busy with, only that he hadn't given up on the project, and that Joey must not lose hope. Joey himself had been occupied full time with cost-cutting, laying off staff, and trying to source other work to keep them afloat. He'd planned to sit down with Khosi and discuss the matter properly, try to convince him that he was wasting his time chasing after the mining deals, and that he should accept defeat and move on.

Perhaps it just got too much for Khosi to handle. If Joey had known—if he'd been able to have that talk with him—he could have intervened. Now, of course, it was too late. He hoisted his rucksack over one shoulder, turned off the light, and closed the front door behind him for the last time.

He stepped into a maelstrom. Rain was sluicing down, drowning out the sound of the traffic. Hailstones pummeled him, ricocheting off the desk's surface. Lightning bathed the street in brilliance, and a heartbeat later, thunder crashed overhead.

A torrent of water was rushing down the side of the road. Well, no way around it, they'd have to get their feet wet to reach the truck—since Joey was already soaked from head to ankles, the thought didn't bother him too much. Just a few more steps and they'd be home and dry.

Suddenly, from behind, somebody shoved him viciously hard. He stumbled forward, losing his grasp on the desk, which thudded down onto the sidewalk. He splashed into the road, arms pinwheeling. Water fountained over him as a passing car swerved violently. Behind him, he heard the truck driver shouting angrily. But before Joey could recover his balance, his rucksack was ripped from his shoulder. A skinny youngster in a black jacket had grabbed it, and was racing away.

CHAPTER 3

THE YOUNGSTER WAS fast, but Joey's swift reflexes helped him recover instantly. Picking himself up, he used the momentum to fling himself forward. With his muscular, broad-shouldered build, he had won rowing championships at college; sprinting had never been his forte, but now his anger lent him wings.

He'd had everything else taken from him in the past few days and he was damned if some crazy mugger was going to get away with this.

As he pounded across the road, he heard the screech of brakes. He glanced to his right to see a minibus taxi hurtling toward him; an ancient-looking death trap of a vehicle. The driver had run the red light and now, too late, he was stamping on worn brakes, as threadbare tires skidded over the wet road. The taxi was hydroplaning, and Joey was directly in its path. The blare of its horn filled the air. He could see its windshield wipers...one moving at full speed, the other hanging down, broken.

Stop, he thought. *Back!*

It was the safest option. But already the skinny youth was sprinting down the opposite sidewalk and if he stopped now, he'd lose him.

Joey decided to make a run for it.

The rear of the taxi was fishtailing…its grille loomed, far too close, and the wailing of worn rubber on tarmac filled his ears. He leaped for the opposite curb, vaulting the crash barrier to safety just as the out-of-control taxi rattled past.

Usually, this sidewalk was cluttered with pedestrians at this time, but today only a few braved the elements, heads bowed under umbrellas and mackintoshes. It was easy to spot the fleeing thief darting between them. It looked as if he was heading for a beaten-up Mazda which had stopped on a yellow line, engine revving.

Frustration surging inside him, Joey realized his assailant had too much of a lead; he wasn't going to catch him in time.

But then the youngster tripped, sprawling to his knees as a cracked manhole lid gave way. He picked himself up and carried on, limping badly, and Joey knew he had a chance.

"Stop!" Joey yelled, racing to intercept the Mazda. The driver was reversing to meet his accomplice. The passenger door swung open and the thief dived in.

But Joey was on him. A desperate lunge, and he had hold of the man's knee, dragging him out again even as the Mazda's driver tried to accelerate away. The thief was clinging to the seat-belt strap, his body in the moving car and his legs scissoring on the asphalt. The Mazda jerked to a stop.

"Give it back!" Joey shouted, twisting the man's left ankle hard. From the screams that followed, he guessed he had gotten hold of the injured leg.

The man kicked out at him wildly with his right foot, but Joey grabbed it with his other hand. He clawed at Joey's head, trying to pull his hair, but Joey's dark buzz cut was too short for him to get a hold. One more powerful yank on the legs, and he pulled the thief right out of the car. He hit the road butt-first, then his head followed with a bump, and finally, his outstretched arms came free. He still held Joey's rucksack in a death grip in his right hand and Joey wrenched it loose.

Street fighting had taught him his skills—crude, but effective. A kick to the crotch, and the thief forgot all about his injured ankle and curled into a ball, his screams turning to sobs.

Lying there in the rain, the young man looked vulnerable and terrified, and Joey suddenly felt sorry for him. He didn't know the would-be mugger's circumstances, but guessed they were even more dire than his own. At any rate, he had his possessions again, and that was what mattered. As the man crawled back to the Mazda, helped in by the visibly shaking driver, Joey shouldered the bag and turned away, jogging down the sidewalk as the rain stung his face.

He passed a streetlight with a newspaper headline poster attached to it. Torn by the wind and ripped by the hail, the print on the paper was illegible apart from a single word at the bottom.

…COINCIDENCE? it read.

Joey looked at the dripping newsprint as he passed, thinking of everything that had happened to him in the recent past. The word stayed in his head, refusing to leave.

He'd sure been unlucky. But had it all been coincidental?

He didn't have Khosi's background as a PI. He'd qualified with a business degree and worked as a forensic analyst in top-level corporate finance. Even so, he should be able to deduce if there was a pattern here, and whether this mugging and the recent burglary were linked.

Damn it, he thought, realizing he shouldn't have let the thief get away without answering some questions. He turned, shielding his eyes against the rain, but the Mazda was gone.

CHAPTER 4

"YOU OKAY?" THE removal-van driver called out from under the shelter of his umbrella, as he saw Joey crossing the road. "Did you catch him?"

"Yes, and yes. I got my bag back," Joey replied, reaching over his shoulder to pat his rucksack. "Let's load up and get out of here."

"Never known crime to be so bad in this neighborhood," the driver said, shaking his head. "Crazy that you can't even walk around safely in broad daylight." He glanced dubiously at the storm clouds, as if unsure whether this awful weather did, in fact, qualify as broad daylight.

Joey gripped the desk again firmly. But as he lifted it, he saw a silvery oval object gleaming on the pavement below.

"Just a sec," he said, because it looked familiar. He bent and picked it up.

He was correct, and his heart quickened as he examined it.

"You dropped it?" the driver asked.

"No, it must have fallen—from somewhere under the desk, I think."

It was Khosi's USB storage device, specially engraved with his name, which Joey had given him as a gift. That had been only three months ago, just before all the trouble started. The device had been attached to a keyring, but Joey saw that the ring had been removed and a piece of double-sided tape attached to it.

Peeling off the tape, he pocketed the USB.

He guessed it had been stuck to the bottom of the desk. If the mugger hadn't shoved Joey off balance and caused him to drop the desk, dislodging the device, then Joey would never have found it. It was sheer luck it had landed on the sidewalk and not in the gutter, to be washed away by the cascading storm water.

Suddenly, Joey shivered, and not just from the chill of the blowing rain.

He was wondering if this USB might contain Khosi's suicide note.

CHAPTER 5

THANKING HIS LUCKY stars that his watch was waterproof, Joey checked the time and saw it had only taken ten minutes to finish loading the office furniture. The attempted mugging hadn't caused too much of a delay.

But there was no time to check the USB he'd picked up. He needed to get to his bodyguarding assignment with Isobel Collins—the sooner, the better.

In the building's small basement garage, he stripped off his soaked shirt and put on a dry one. He always kept a change of clothes in the trunk of his SUV, because investigation work was unpredictable. In the past, he'd often had to drive straight from a dirty, dusty site to a boardroom meeting. Today, he was especially thankful he'd packed a fresh pair of shoes and socks. His gym bag with the change of clothes was packed next to the other essentials in the Private Johannesburg world—cable ties, duct tape, rope, bottled water, and a knife.

Then he set off, joining the Friday rush-hour traffic heading out of the city center and onto the highway going east.

As soon as he got onto the road, he called Jack Morgan on his cell phone.

Jack seemed to travel almost nonstop. When Joey had phoned to break the news of Khosi's death, Jack had been in Paris, on his way to board a plane to New York. In the few seconds this call took to connect, Joey had time to wonder in which country, and which continent, Private's owner would be now.

"Joey." Jack answered after just one ring, sounding concerned. "You doing okay?"

"It's tough at the moment, but I'm coping," Joey replied. "I'm on my way to a bodyguarding assignment. It's the first time I've done this. I thought it would be routine, that it was just a tourist needing some extra security. But the lady sounds scared, and she's staying in a very dangerous part of the city. I don't know why she's there. Don't know if it's my job to ask questions."

Jack was silent for a moment, and Joey was sure he heard a seagull calling in the background.

"As a professional, your job is to assess the risks and threats effectively," Jack said eventually. "Ask all the questions you need to in order to do that, and continually assess your surroundings. Circumstances can change very quickly in those situations, so keep your eyes open."

"I will," Joey promised.

"And remember, whatever she's there for, your role as a close-protection officer isn't to get in her way or try to stop her, it's to keep her safe while she does it."

"Thanks, Jack. Appreciate the help."

"All the best with it, and call me if you need anything else."

"I will." Putting his phone down, Joey accelerated through a gap in the traffic, heading to his assignment with a renewed sense of purpose.

CHAPTER 6

"**WHAT THE HELL** have I gotten myself into?" Isobel Collins muttered to herself. Frowning through the downpour, she inched her rental car down the road, which was studded with potholes. Hopefully she would spot a house number at some stage. The people living here didn't seem to be into numbering their homes. Or repairing their crumbling walls, or replacing broken window glass.

She'd been driving for what felt like hours through torrential rain. She was already feeling seriously out of her depth, and not just because the roads were starting to flood.

The person sitting next to her on the plane had been a friendly fashion designer who'd raved about Johannesburg's buzz and energy. He'd told her about the inner city's upliftment project, the thriving markets, the music scene and the arts and crafts venues. Then he'd written out a list of trendy bars and restaurants that she simply had to visit during her stay.

But while she'd been waiting at baggage reclaim, she'd spoken to a grim-faced woman heading back to see her elderly parents. She'd been shocked to hear Isobel was traveling alone. She warned her that the country was going to the dogs, crime was out of control in Johannesburg, and that her father had recently been robbed at gunpoint while walking across the road to the grocery store.

Which one of them to believe?

On arrival at O.R. Tambo International Airport, she'd been reassured by how modern, pristine, and efficient it was, bustling with a diversity of visitors. However, her confidence had evaporated as she'd left the airport and driven into the bleak outskirts of Johannesburg, with views of heavy machinery and mine dumps dimly visible from the highway. Now, the area where she was heading was far more run-down than she'd expected. The housing ranged from dilapidated dwellings to tin-roofed shacks; the metal rattling and banging in the wind.

Isobel reached a building with a high precast concrete wall that she assumed to be her lodgings. It was the only place she'd been able to find in the area, and now she could see why travelers' accommodations were so scarce.

Fear simmered deep within her and she tried to subdue it by humming to herself as she parked outside, pretending that everything was okay. That she was used to traveling alone in strange countries where violent crime was rife. That she hadn't made a huge error of judgment in coming here at all, which was confirmed by the fact that she'd not realized she was overnighting in a slum.

The front door wobbled on its hinges; its battered surface made her think someone had once tried to kick their way in. After she knocked, it was opened by an elderly woman in a gray smock.

"Power's out," the woman muttered. Before Isobel could gather her thoughts, she'd handed her the key, opened her umbrella, and set off down the road.

"Well, I'll bring my own bags in," Isobel shouted after her, angrily brushing water from her short blond hair. Her annoyance at this rudeness did little to budge the coldness that had settled in her stomach. She was completely alone here. Apart from Joey Montague, only one person knew exactly where she was staying—her friend Samantha, back in the States, who had helped her organize this secret mission.

Once inside, between the crashes of thunder, she heard a persistent tapping sound. She discovered it was water, dripping down onto the tiled floor from a leak in the roof.

Her smart crimson luggage looked out of place when she set the bags down in the gloomy hallway. She locked the front door before taking them to the bedroom. Closing the bedroom door made the room even darker, but seemed like the safer option, even though it didn't have a lock.

The place smelled dusty and disused, and she found her toes reflexively curling as she looked at the narrow single bed, with its dented mattress, gray pillowcase, and threadbare coverlet.

You are just a spoiled princess who's forgotten how most of the world lives, she chided herself. Since she'd met her husband five years ago, she'd only traveled in luxury, because Dave was a wealthy man. She'd become used to palatial accommodations, crisp white sheets, five-star service.

We won't be able to afford those hotels for much longer, unless I can work out what the hell's going on here, Isobel told herself.

She unzipped the compartment of her bag and took out the notebook where she'd written the findings of her investigation. In the very front of it, she'd noted down the coordinates she needed. They were nearby—this was why she'd chosen these lodgings—and she took a deep, shaky breath at the thought that she was finally so close.

She didn't need to look in her book, because she'd memorized the coordinates: 26 degrees, 14 minutes, 48 seconds south; 28 degrees, 13 minutes, 18 seconds east.

She checked the time on her cell phone, and compared it again with the calculations she had made in her notebook. Nervousness clenched her stomach as she realized she'd need to be at this location in two hours. After weeks of waiting, it suddenly seemed like a very tight deadline, and she hoped that Mr. Montague would arrive before she had to leave, because if he didn't, she had no idea what she'd do.

You'll have to go on your own, she thought. *Can't be worse than staying here, can it?*

Well, actually, she wasn't convinced about that, because she would be venturing into the unknown. The only certainty was the place marked by the coordinates…she had no idea what she would find there.

"Twenty-six degrees south," she said out loud, wishing she felt braver.

And then another crash from outside the bedroom made her jump.

That wasn't thunder. It sounded different, and closer… much closer. Isobel eased open the bedroom door and peered out.

CHAPTER 7

THE STORM HAD made the Friday afternoon traffic worse. Much worse. From personal experience, Joey knew Johannesburg drivers fell into two categories. Some of them believed a storm meant they should drive at top speed to try and outrun the rain. The others believed they should stop dead in their tracks at the first sign of a storm, and wait the weather out.

The problems occurred when the two categories of driver collided.

It took Joey twenty minutes to struggle past numerous bumper-bashings onto the highway, only to discover that an earlier accident had caused a massive tailback. The blare of horns provided a continuous soundtrack to the frustrating conditions.

Waiting in an immobile queue of cars, Joey tried to call Isobel to reassure her he'd be there soon, but he couldn't connect to her number. Perhaps she'd turned her phone off, but he thought it was more likely the storm had wiped out cell signals in that area. Whatever the reason, it meant he had no way of getting hold of her at all.

He forced himself to relax his grip on the wheel, telling himself that worrying was counterproductive. He could only hope that she had also been delayed and wasn't sitting alone in her lodgings, vulnerable and afraid.

To help calm himself, he glanced down at the photo on his phone's screen: a beautiful young woman with green eyes and dark hair. His fifteen-year-old daughter, Hayley, had inherited his coloring and his height, but he wasn't sure where she'd gotten her love of storms and thunder. And heavy metal, and anything loud.

She was his favorite person in the world, and she had just moved to Cape Town with his ex-wife. She'd planned to travel to Jo'burg to do intern work for Private in her school holidays. He'd been looking forward to it. But with everything that had happened recently, and the trouble the business was in, he guessed it would be better for Hayley to stay in Cape Town with her mother.

The last time he'd seen her, she'd pranked him by setting his phone's ringtone to Metallica's "Fade to Black." He'd kept it, because it reminded him of her. Now, the tune started playing loudly.

"Montague speaking," he said.

"Joey? It's Paul Du Preez." He recognized the voice of the pathologist who was doing Khosi's autopsy.

"Paul. Is there any news?" he asked, surprised. The mortuaries were so crowded that it usually took weeks to obtain results.

"No, the autopsy's scheduled for next Friday. But I drew blood when the body was signed in and sent it for testing."

"Is that usual?"

"You know Khosi was a good friend of mine. Just last week we sat down for a beer together and he didn't seem depressed."

"I didn't think so, either," Joey admitted.

"I did a quick examination when the body came in. There was a spot of blood on his pants and a tiny hole in the fabric."

"Serious?" Joey gripped the wheel so tightly his fingers hurt.

"When I took a closer look, there were clear signs of a needle prick on the back of the thigh. So I took blood, and submitted the samples. I'm waiting for the results, which should come back this evening. If they're positive, the police are going to want to interview you again."

"You sure about the needle prick?" Joey asked, astonished. Khosi had been tough, alert, and experienced. He wouldn't have submitted to an injection without fighting hard.

"I'm certain," Paul confirmed. He added, as if reading Joey's mind, "I didn't pick up any visible signs of defensive injuries. But in the back of the thigh like that, an intramuscular shot would be fast and easy to do, and would take effect within a minute or two."

"So you think trickery, rather than force?"

He imagined Paul nodding, his lips pressed together as he did when thinking hard.

"Yes. I would say it's more likely. Trickery, distraction, something like that. But until we get the results back, it's all hypothesizing." The line started to crackle as the rain worsened again.

"We'll speak later," Joey said, and disconnected, his mind reeling from this latest bombshell.

There had been foul play involved; the suicide was not, in fact, what it seemed. That word he saw on the poster, COINCIDENCE?, had stuck in his mind for a reason; his subconscious had known what he'd been too shocked to consciously understand.

CHAPTER 8

ISOBEL DISCOVERED THE lounge window had made the crashing noise. Loose in its frame, it had slammed so hard that a pane of glass had fallen out and smashed on the floor. The wind was howling through the gap, billowing out the dirty net curtain and sending rain spattering over the tiles.

"Hell!" Isobel pushed the bedroom door wide and ran over to the disaster zone. The thin soles of her trainers crunched on broken glass. Reaching for the window, she found she couldn't close it properly; the wooden frame had warped, and she was unable to pull it hard enough. The wind snatched it right out of her grasp and slammed it again. There were five panes left in the window, one had cracked, and another two looked loose.

"Oh, damn it!" Isobel shouted. She needed to do some urgent damage control. What would happen if the window broke completely? Scenarios spun through her head, each more chilling than the last, underpinned by the fear that she might have to spend the night here alone.

Perhaps pushing the window back into its frame from the outside would be easier than pulling from the inside. Isobel rushed back into the bedroom, unzipped her suitcase, and grabbed the colorful red-and-white floral raincoat that Dave had given her for Christmas. Like all of Dave's gifts, it was top-of-the-line, a designer garment. Hastily, she pulled it on.

She unlocked the front door and stepped into the gusting rain. Turning, she locked it behind her. It felt like a paranoid action, considering she was only going to be in the garden for a few minutes, but she couldn't risk leaving it open. The warning from the woman at the baggage reclaim kept playing in her head. *"These robbers watch the homes closely. They wait for a chance, and then they attack. All it takes is one careless moment."*

Better to be careful, especially with her instincts prickling. Isobel pocketed the key and sprinted around the house.

She grabbed the window frame to steady herself. The rain hammered on the tin roof, streaming off its edge and splattering directly onto her head. Shaking it away, she focused on the task at hand. Lifting the window would fit it back into the frame, and then she could wedge it all the way shut. Of course, the unwelcome truth was that it would be just as easy to force open again, especially with one missing pane. But if she closed it tightly enough, maybe she could find some wire or twine to secure it from the inside.

Isobel grasped the window and lifted it, pressing her face against the murky pane as she maneuvered the frame into place. For a heart-stopping moment, she thought she saw movement inside the room. She drew in a fast breath, blinking water out of her eyes and telling herself not to be stupid. It was nothing more than the rain on glass, which was also causing the optical illusion that light was coming in through the closed front door.

The window slotted back into place with a bang, but horror gripped her as she stared into the house.

No illusion, no mistake. Impossibly, her fears had become reality.

The front door was open, and a tall, lean man was moving stealthily toward the bedroom. He was dressed in black, wearing a beanie. He must have heard the sound the window made, because he turned to face her. It was then Isobel saw the unmistakable shape of the gun in his hand.

CHAPTER 9

SHOCK SLOWED ISOBEL'S reactions. It was only when the tall man raised his weapon that her astonished brain caught up. She dove down, sprawling on all fours in the muddy water, as two shots exploded through the glass above her.

Go! Go! She had no idea whether she was screaming out loud or in her head, but she knew that running for her life, as far and fast as she could, was her only option.

Which way? Adrenaline pumped through her veins, quickening her decisions as she jumped to her feet. Back the way she'd come? He'd catch her at the front door. Straight out the gate? No; she could see a car hood there, and what if there was a second man inside?

Only one choice left...over the wall.

She raced to the precast concrete barrier and launched herself at it in a desperate leap. The rough surface snagged the raincoat, ripping the sleeve open and grazing her skin, but she didn't notice it. Her arms shook with the effort; she'd been neglecting the gym in recent weeks and spending time on her investigations instead. Using all her strength, tendons burning, she hauled herself higher and hooked an elbow over the top. A final scramble and she had made it. She flung herself over, slamming down onto the pavement before struggling to her feet again.

Where to now? The instinct to flee overrode all logical decision-making. In a blind panic, she veered down a narrow side street, but found it offered no cover. On either side of the road was empty ground with sparse grass that wasn't long enough to hide in.

Farther ahead, she saw rows of shacks, patched together from corrugated steel and uneven bricks. In the rain, she had no idea if they were empty, abandoned, or occupied…but they were her only chance. If she could reach the shacks in time, there might be somebody who could help, and at the very least, she could duck out of sight and maybe even lose him there.

But then, behind her, she heard the sound she'd dreaded…the roar of a powerful engine and the splash of tires, coming fast toward her.

CHAPTER 10

SOME PEOPLE WERE born with natural beauty, or musical ability, or a photographic memory. Steyn had a different talent. He was gifted with the ability to kill. Not just to commit the act of murder, although this was an exceptional skill that few people could carry out in cold blood…but to create a plausible scenario for each job he did.

He liked to think of it as helping the police. After all, with South Africa's high crime rate, they were all overworked and demoralized. Making their task easier saved on paperwork and time, freeing them up to hunt down criminals more careless than him.

He always did his homework carefully. It was essential to be properly prepared. After all, the more time he took over the preparation, the less time the detectives would need to work out what had occurred.

And, of course, he always had a backup plan. Having a Plan B was absolutely essential.

When he swiftly forced the front door of Isobel's lodgings

and moved calmly into the house, nothing about his demeanor gave away the fact that this was already Plan B. His lean face was intent, and the hand holding his pistol was steady.

Plan A had been to do the job on the road, to make it look as though the woman had been shot in a carjacking. However, the rainy weather put an end to that. No carjacker would work in such a storm. With the heavy traffic and poor visibility, there was too much risk of a botched getaway. So, thinking like the criminal he was, albeit a different kind of criminal, Steyn had decided on his second plan. After all, a violent house robbery would be nothing unusual in this impoverished community. The word could easily have spread that an overseas traveler was booked in.

Steyn's instincts were already telling him the house was empty when he heard the window slam. Spinning around, he saw her looking in, and suddenly the scenario made sense— she'd gone out to try and close it.

He fired two shots, but to his annoyance she was quicker than he'd expected; he would have thought she'd freeze, cry, beg for her life, as most of his female victims had done.

Quickly, he strode outside. The chase was on now, and he didn't intend to lose. At such moments, he always smiled, the left side of his mouth quirking up; but it was a joker's grin that never reached his eyes.

Gun at the ready, he moved to the corner of the house, blinking rain away. She would be crouching down, on the ground—he aimed low, then rounded the corner.

Another shock…she wasn't there. In fact, she was nowhere in sight. Could she have hidden? The overgrown garden, small as it was, offered some opportunities. He was about to search through the bushes, but then remembered the flash of red he'd caught as she ducked down behind the window. A bright garment like she was wearing would be visible; she couldn't hope to hide. Implacably, the computer in Steyn's mind came up with another solution and he scanned the area. His mouth curved higher as he saw it.

There, on the wall.

A fluttering swatch of red-and-white material, tugged by the wind.

She'd gone over, and would be fleeing down the side street, the one with all the shacks.

Steyn ran for his car. A moment later, he was accelerating around the corner, tires wailing.

CHAPTER 11

ISOBEL RACED DOWN the narrow road. Her legs were pumping, her lungs burned, the stupid raincoat was flapping, its brightness a beacon that was guiding him to her. She couldn't outrun her terror—fear consumed her, but at the same time, she knew she had nothing to lose in trying anything that might buy her an extra few seconds.

If she could reach the shacks, she'd have a chance. In the maze of tin roofs and tumbledown walls she could lose her pursuer and they would shield her from his bullets. If she screamed now, could anyone hear her?

But she was still too far away, and she knew that meant she'd never reach the shacks. The car was catching up too fast. The engine's roar filled her ears. What would the shot feel like, when it came? She felt a burning in the small of her back, where she expected the bullet to hit.

And then the car pulled level.

"Isobel?" the driver shouted.

The urgency in his voice made her turn to look. This car

wasn't the silvery sedan whose hood she'd seen. It was a big black SUV with the driver's window all the way open. She could see there was only one person in the car, and it wasn't her would-be killer. This man was tanned and tough-looking, with close-cropped dark hair.

"Get in, quick," he urged her, and the passenger door swung open as the car skidded to a stop. "I'm Joey Montague."

CHAPTER 12

IT HAD BEEN pure luck that Joey had driven that way; he knew the area and he remembered the shortcut from the highway. He'd thought the advantages of the shorter route would outweigh the fact that it was a terrible road.

When he saw the woman sprinting through the heavy rain, her red-patterned raincoat flapping behind her, he guessed it had to be Isobel, and that something was wrong. Instead of driving straight to the house where she was staying, he swung the car left and sped after her.

Now, ten seconds later, his new client had collapsed on the car's passenger seat, gasping, "Get out…of here. He's chasing…me."

"Who?" Joey was already accelerating away, checking his mirrors to see if anyone was following.

"I…don't know. He broke into…the house."

"What did he look like?"

"Tall, thin, wearing…a black beanie and carrying a gun."

"Did you see a vehicle?"

"Silver sedan. Not sure…what make."

Checking his rearview mirror again, Joey felt a coldness in his stomach as he saw that a silver BMW had turned onto the road.

"Fasten your seat belt," he told her. This pursuit was likely to be dangerous.

CHAPTER 13

JOEY SLALOMED THE car through the potholes. A crossroads ahead...at this hour, it was usually quiet. Taking the gamble, he barely touched the brakes before speeding through. Even though he was using every skill he had, he was aware with every passing second that his heavy SUV was not ideal for the job.

His firearm was holstered under his jacket, but it wouldn't do him much good at this moment. Trying to use it would be dangerous, ineffective, and would slow them down. For now, he needed to concentrate on his driving, because the BMW following was faster and more agile, and it was gaining ground.

"He's catching up!" Twisted around in her seat, Isobel helpfully informed him of the obvious.

"I know."

"Can you go faster?"

"If I could, I would."

"Maybe there's...a side street, or something?" But her

voice lost hope as the road unrolled ahead, devoid of intersections.

"There's one at the top of the hill!" Her tone brightened.

"We want to avoid that. It's a dead end."

"You know this place so well?"

"Like the back of my hand. We recently did a major assignment in this area."

Joey checked his mirrors again and saw how much ground the BMW had gained. The driver had both hands on the wheel, his face drawn into the rictus of a grin. He was taking his time before shooting, knowing his quarry was trapped on the road and all out of options.

But time for him also meant time for them, and suddenly Joey realized where they could go.

Parallel to this road was a dirt track that led to one of the vulnerable mine entrances where Private had placed security guards. Once before, in better weather, he'd managed to cross the veldt and access that road. In this weather, it would be a huge gamble, but there was one certainty he could rely on.

The SUV would get farther than the low-slung sedan behind them.

"Hang on tight," he warned Isobel.

She glanced at him, blue eyes wide, her short, platinum hair in spiky disarray.

"To what?" she asked him breathlessly.

"To whatever you can find. We're heading off-road."

A final glance in the mirror. He was only just in time. The

man behind was right on their tail now. His window was open and he was ready to shoot.

Wrenching the wheel to the right, Joey stood on the brakes.

The tires screamed as the big vehicle slewed sideways. Joey fought the wheel, aware that Isobel had grabbed the dash with one hand, and his shoulder with the other. He'd swerved right to avoid a collision with the car pursuing them, hoping the BMW would accelerate ahead, but he hadn't bargained on their hunter reacting so fast. A second shriek of tires told him he hadn't gained any ground from this maneuver. That damned kidney grille was still looming behind them.

Joey scanned the embankment, desperately looking for a place to turn that wouldn't gut the car instantly. There…the ground was more even in a spot just ahead. Not much smoother, but enough to give them a chance.

"*Now* try and follow us," Joey snapped. He swung the wheel, and the big SUV sped over the embankment. There was a harsh scraping sound, which he'd expected, but the rain worked in their favor, softening the ground so that the heavy vehicle plowed through the top of the bank, instead of getting stuck. Then they were airborne, and Isobel's grip on his shoulder tightened. They landed with a stomach-wrenching thud, and went bouncing across the muddy veldt beyond.

A whiplash crack from behind, and a hole punched through the middle of the windshield. A few inches left or right, and one of them would be dead.

"Down," Joey urged. Isobel, face white, flattened herself. He couldn't risk doing the same—this going was treacherous and there was too much risk of hitting a rock or ending up in a ditch. He swerved around a massive termite mound jutting out of long grass that could hide other obstacles.

Another shot from behind, but this one went wide. Now, every second that passed took them farther out of range. In his mirrors, he saw the tall man, standing at the top of the embankment. Realizing he couldn't follow them, the man had climbed out of his car to get a better shot.

Then Joey glanced at Isobel. She was sitting up again, even though he hadn't told her to. On her face, he saw only fierce concentration, and felt a sudden surge of admiration for her toughness, which he hadn't expected.

"Ditch on the left," she warned, and he altered course to avoid a gaping channel in the ground, well camouflaged by overgrowth.

"By the way," she added, "thank you for saving my life."

"I was only just in time," Joey said. "Whoever was chasing us is a professional, for sure, and he will still be on the hunt. So, tell me what's going on. What kind of trouble have you gotten yourself into?"

CHAPTER 14

IT WAS UNUSUAL for Steyn to be frustrated. But now, he felt his control slipping away. Standing in the mud and staring at the SUV's receding brake lights, he clenched his fists as pure, killing rage overwhelmed him.

She'd escaped again. Who had picked her up? Her bodyguard had been canceled—he had made sure of that. But someone had rescued her, and random knights in shining armor were in short supply around here. So she must have booked somebody else. With this man's help, she had outwitted him.

Breathing hard, he stared into the rain until the SUV disappeared from view. He was soaking wet. His beanie was drenched. He ripped it off and shook out his brown hair, cut into a neat and unremarkable style.

His nails dug into his palms as he imagined the woman—overpowered at last, perhaps injured, but not yet dead. She'd bested him, and that was unforgivable. It was seldom Steyn had the opportunity to exact a slow revenge. But now he promised her silently: *When I find you—not if, when—I will not give you the mercy of a quick death.*

It had been a long time since he'd been able to have his own way with a victim. In jobs, the clients' needs came first, and a faster killing was less risky. He'd had the opportunity last year, a happy accident of timing, and he could remember every moment. The victim had lasted for thirteen hours and eight minutes before he'd died. As Steyn had listened to his screams hoarsen and fade, and watched the man's struggles slowly weaken under his ministrations, Steyn had felt something inside him slowly release, unfolding into warmth. He very seldom had feelings of joy. Anger, occasionally. Fear, never. His only fear was being confined. He wasn't sure why, but suspected it was to do with his early childhood, of which he had only vague memories and occasional nightmares.

Now, remembering that rare surge of pleasure, he managed to calm himself again. There would be time. Later, he promised himself, there would be time. If not for the woman, then for the man. He might not know now who Isobel's rescuer was, but Steyn could easily find out. He had a wide network of connections in government departments. Information was a currency, one he traded in frequently. He occasionally paid bribes, but preferred to offer a monthly retainer to key people in exchange for their services.

And for now, his thoughts were clear again, logic slicing cleanly through the emotion and allowing him to formulate a new plan. There could be only one place where his target, and her mysterious Good Samaritan, were headed. After all, it was where he expected her to go. They were taking the back route, a slow, tortuous journey through mired dirt roads. Steyn could take the highway; a longer drive, but so much faster. In fact, it would leave him time for an important detour along the way.

"I'm coming for you," he murmured.

Then he climbed into the BMW and carefully backed it off the muddy verge. Speed was not his friend here…the tires needed time to bite and grip. A minute later, and he was safely back on the road.

Soon afterward, he was back at Isobel's rental house. His mouth twisted in amusement as he walked inside. What she must have thought, arriving here…a spoiled, wealthy housewife. He doubted she'd dreamed she would find herself in such a place. There was her luggage in the bedroom: a beautiful set of Louis Vuitton bags. It was ideal for his purposes. He would need it when he created the scenario surrounding her death.

One of the bags was unzipped, and a small notebook filled with neat handwriting lay on top of the folded clothes. Steyn removed it before closing the bag, and slipped it into his jacket pocket, in case it contained anything useful.

Picking up the bags, Steyn mused over the challenge of making the woman's death slow, rather than swift. It might be best to plant the bags and the car somewhere and have her simply vanish. A missing person. Perhaps he could drop some clues surrounding her disappearance—a few key items removed from the suitcases, to hint at the fact that she might have purposely disappeared. The police wouldn't look as hard if they suspected she was a runaway.

Once he'd had his pleasure with her, he would dump her body. He had the ideal location in mind already: a large piece of open ground in Johannesburg's sought-after northern suburbs. It had recently been bought for development but, as yet, the property was unsecured. A sewer line ran through it. Built in the early 1900s, it was still in use today. The brick-and-mortar tunnel was high and wide enough to easily accommodate a body, and Steyn had recently read an article stating that the manhole covers in that area were continually being stolen for their scrap-metal value.

Johannesburg's sewer system was under enormous pressure as a result of the city's recent growth. Blockages—if they occurred—were often left unattended for weeks or months. If Isobel's body was ever discovered, it would be thoroughly rotted and completely unrecognizable. Nothing would ever link those corrupted remains back to Steyn.

Mulling over his plan, he walked back to the hallway, but when he reached the front door, it was snatched open from the outside before he could touch the handle.

Steyn found himself staring at an overweight, angry-looking stranger. Shaven-headed, he wore a black vest that showed the tattoos on his neck and chest, and the bulky muscles of his arms and shoulders.

"What's going on?" the large man demanded. "I live down the road. I heard shooting and a woman's screams coming from this house awhile ago. Where's the lady? Were you fighting?"

Looking at the stranger's hands, Steyn saw he was carrying a Taser in his right hand and a large knife in his left.

CHAPTER 15

ISOBEL RAN AN impatient hand through her blond hair, slicking back the damp spikes. "There's a saying about good intentions. How does it go?" she asked.

"Supposedly, the road to hell is paved with them," Joey said, a flicker of amusement easing the knots of stress in his belly as he reached the dirt track and joined it, heading east. The rain was easing up now, although drizzle still misted the windshield.

"Yes, that sums it up, I guess. Pretty much feels like I'm on the road to hell, right here." Isobel stared ahead at the muddy pathway, stretching to a gray and forbidding horizon. "In fact, I might even know the coordinates for hell itself. Twenty-six degrees south, twenty-eight degrees east. I've got the full details written down, and memorized. They're where I need to be, at 6:00 p.m. But I think I'm going to be too late, and in any case, I don't have any cell phone signal so I can't use the GPS."

"This is a dead zone for signal. It might come back after

we've passed that mine dump up ahead. But we're heading in the right direction, I think."

"You really do know this area well."

"My firm had contracts all over the East Rand, which is where we are now."

Isobel paused for a beat. When she spoke again, she sounded confused.

"You said 'had contracts.' Are they over?"

"Unfortunately, yes. They were canceled due to circumstances beyond our control."

"That must have been a blow," Isobel sympathized.

"It was," Joey said. Briefly, he told Isobel about the hard work it had taken to start up Private Johannesburg; the many nights when he'd arrived home close to midnight, leaving again before the sun was up. That was the problem with investigation work—the hours were punishingly long. His frequent absences had recently cost him his marriage. Although, to be brutally honest, he and his wife, Anneke, had been drifting apart for years.

"I proposed marriage after Anneke got pregnant when we were dating," he told Isobel, knowing it was probably way too much information, but the way she was listening was encouraging him to talk. "It seemed like the biggest catastrophe of my life at the time, but it turned into the most incredible miracle when my daughter, Hayley, was born."

"How old is she now?"

"Fifteen. She's just moved to Cape Town. I'm missing her

terribly," he confessed. "But anyway, back to the business. Private Johannesburg's first major assignment was with the gold mines in this area, offering a full-service investigation and security solution."

"Oh, really? What did that involve?"

"We worked with various mining sites both operational and closed. They needed help because there's a huge problem with illegal mining in Johannesburg, particularly on the East Rand. We were hired to investigate and to protect. To identify areas at risk, place guards at vulnerable entrances, track down the kingpins, get them arrested, and prevent it from happening again."

"Illegal mining?"

"It's a crime that's rife here at the moment, especially on Johannesburg's East Rand, where we are now. People see gold as a promise of wealth. And knowing that ore-rich rock is available can prove a huge temptation if you're poor, or desperate, or happen to be a criminal. It's not difficult to do, because mines often cover huge tracts of land and existing entrances can be closed for many reasons. Perhaps the ore is no longer commercially viable, or the seam has become too dangerous to mine. That's when the zama zamas—the illegal miners—move in."

"Then what happens?" Isobel's eyes were wide. Joey noticed they were a clear, light blue in color.

"Only bad things. For a start, the operations are usually run by gangs, headed up by anonymous criminal kingpins. The workers go underground for days at a time, and because there are no regulations in place, they risk injury or death from rock collapses and suffocation. There's also the constant threat of violence from other illegal miners working for opposing gangs."

"That's terrible!"

"They're a huge threat to the legitimate mining industry, and in areas where zama zamas operate, the levels of serious crime always shoot through the roof."

"So what forced you to stop your investigation?" Isobel asked. Joey saw that her stressed expression had eased and her features looked lively and animated. Painful as the story was, he was glad that it was providing her, and him, with a distraction from the terror they'd just endured.

"Government policy killed us," he said, and felt sadness weighing him down.

"How?"

"Mr. Mashabela, the minister of mineral and energy affairs, made a law banning mines from hiring private investigators and security."

"But that's crazy! Why did he do that?"

"He said he intended to deploy the Hawks to investigate the problem—they're a special branch of the police service that deals with organized crime. He believed hiring private security would be too risky for the mines and that, instead, he would allocate police to guard the necessary entrances."

"And did he?"

Joey sighed. "Months have gone by since his decision. The Hawks are still not on the case, and no police have been deployed. Crime is escalating, and a number of zama zama gangs are already back in operation."

"That must have been a huge blow to you."

"It was. We'd invested everything into these contracts, and believed they were watertight. The change in government policy blindsided us all—the mines, and Private Johannesburg. We all suffered as a result. Some of the mines have had to close up or scale down as well."

"Joey, that's awful."

"It's life." He gave her a forced smile. "There will be other opportunities, once I've gotten through this." He found he couldn't tell her about Khosi's death. Right then, it was too painful to say the words. He needed to read whatever might be on the USB device, which felt as if it was burning a hole in his pocket.

Quickly, he changed the subject.

"See that reddish strip of ground up ahead? That's the dirt road. We're nearly there. So enough of my story, now. I want to hear yours. Where are we going, and why? What sort of hell are your good intentions leading us to?"

"I have absolutely no idea," Isobel admitted.

"No idea at all?" Eyebrows raised, Joey turned to stare at her. He hoped she was joking, but as soon as he saw her face, he realized she was deadly serious.

"I googled the coordinates, and all they show is a couple of narrow tracks crisscrossing empty land. I don't know if there's something on site which isn't visible, or whether it's used as a meeting point."

Forging ahead into unknown peril. They were in bigger trouble than Joey thought.

CHAPTER 16

JOEY DROVE IN silence for a while as he absorbed Isobel's latest bombshell. They were heading into an unknown situation, armed with only one pistol and a set of coordinates.

"That's why I came to South Africa," she added, sounding apologetic. "Because I'm hoping to find out."

With so few facts available, Joey thought Isobel might have been wiser to hire a small army when she arrived at O.R. Tambo International, instead of putting her trust in just one bodyguard.

"Well, what do you know so far?" Joey asked. "Start from the beginning, and let's see how much we can piece together."

"My husband, Dave, runs a road-freight company. I'm here because of him," Isobel said.

Joey was surprised by the stab of disappointment he felt when he heard her mention a husband. It wasn't until that moment he noticed the large, marquise-cut diamond on her wedding finger. Usually, his first advice to tourists traveling in dangerous areas was to remove visible jewelry and hide it away. But perhaps now wasn't the right time to suggest this, he thought.

"Why didn't he come with you?" Joey asked, wondering if Dave had any idea of the danger she was facing, and if so, why he'd let her travel alone.

"Let me give you some background," Isobel said. "Dave expanded his business into Africa two and a half years ago. Since then, he's been making out as if everything's fine, and that business has never been better. We've been taking luxury vacations, and he bought us each a new Porsche Cayenne last Christmas. He's building a vacation home in the Hamptons and my birthday present this year was a stunning pink diamond eternity necklace, set in platinum."

"Wow," Joey said, and Isobel nodded before continuing.

"I didn't know there was a problem at all. Dave doesn't discuss business with me. But one of my good friends, Samantha, works for his company, managing the accounts. When I showed her my necklace, she looked worried, instead of pleased, and sort of blurted out that she wondered how much it had cost. Anyway, we ended up going for coffee on the weekend and she confessed to me that she was really worried, because it looked like the company was in big trouble financially. She assumed Dave had told me, but he hadn't said a word. I mean, he was acting completely normal." Isobel rolled her eyes. "If you define 'normal' as hosting business lunches at Masa twice a week and flying his helicopter to the Hamptons every weekend for site meetings with his architect," she added.

Joey noted that Isobel hadn't included herself in either of the activities. Briefly, he wondered how happy their marriage was.

"What do you mean by financial trouble?" he asked. "Did Samantha explain?"

Isobel nodded. "Turnover has halved in the past year. Dave has been focusing on the African network and neglecting the US side of the business. The US business has shrunk substantially, and the African network, which started out profitable, is now in the red and hemorrhaging costs."

"Did you discuss it with Dave?"

"Yes. I tried to talk to him about it many times. But every time he became angry and just shut down, refusing to listen."

Joey glanced at Isobel again, but she was looking down at her hands, twisting the ring back and forth.

"He's like that," she added, as if trying to apologize for him. "He's a proud man. I don't think he would ever admit to needing help. So I decided I was going to try to help him anyway. Samantha and I started an in-depth investigation."

"What did you find?"

"The African network manager was replaced thirteen months ago, and very soon after that, profits started to fall. The new manager, Brogan, is an old friend of Dave's, and to be honest, I've never liked him. Or trusted him."

Joey could feel his skin prickling, sensing trouble.

"And then we discovered something else. The new information turned out to be a game-changer. It was the reason I decided to travel out here and see what I could find at these coordinates." Isobel checked her phone again. "Oh, look, I've got a signal back again. And we're heading in the right direction. We should arrive there in ten minutes—wherever 'there' is—so we'll be in time."

"Don't speak too soon," Joey warned, easing the car down a steep slope and tightening his lips as he saw the road disappear into a churned sea of mud. Even in dry weather, this part of the drive was treacherous. In wet weather, it was occasionally impassable, but backtracking would take too long, and it was already starting to get dark. He could only hope that they'd be lucky this time.

They weren't.

The wheels slipped and spun as the SUV failed to gain traction to climb out of the ravine. The big car wallowed in the deep mud, its forward momentum bleeding away. They were stuck, unable to go forward or back, the tires spinning helplessly in the mire.

CHAPTER 17

"WHERE'S THE LADY?" the angry man repeated, blocking Steyn's way out of the front door and fixing him with a glare.

Steyn took a cool, unemotional look at his adversary. He noted the tightness of his grip on the Taser and the aggressive set of his jaw. Undoubtedly, this man was wired for action, and wouldn't hesitate to use one of his two weapons.

Steyn's gun was holstered out of sight, under his rain jacket.

Even without his firearm, Steyn knew he was more than capable of disarming and killing this amateur. Given time, Steyn would have enjoyed using both the man's weapons against him. But right now, he didn't have the luxury of time. Killing could be done quickly, but disposing of the body would take longer.

He decided that, in this case, talking his way out of the situation would work best. Of course, there was a chance that Mr. Taser wouldn't believe him, and in that case he'd go ahead with Plan B.

Depending on his reaction to Steyn, the angry man would be choosing to live or die, without even knowing it.

There was a poetic justice to this that Steyn found pleasing.

"The lady is in the bathroom. She needs a few minutes alone to stop crying and pull herself together before we leave," he said, injecting a strong London accent into his voice and making sure it quivered with emotion. Raising his voice, he called out, "It's okay, darling. It's just a neighbor who heard the shots. Take your time. I'll be there in a minute."

He turned back to the visitor. "We're getting out of this hellhole—we were totally misled. It was supposed to be safe, secure accommodation in a quiet area." He snorted. "Never believe what you read on a website. I'll be telling TripAdvisor about this as soon as we get back home. I never, ever want to go through such horror again. I can't believe we're still alive."

Emotions flickered over Mr. Taser's face. Aggression was replaced first by doubt, and then by curiosity.

"What happened?"

"We were attacked by armed robbers. Two of them, both carrying guns. They must have followed us from the airport…I tried to check my mirrors as you're supposed to do, but in the rain…" He shrugged. "I guess it made it easy for them. We locked ourselves in when we arrived, not that it made a difference." He glanced at the broken lock. "We'd just started unpacking when we heard the noise. We weren't sure what it was. Susan thought it was somebody knocking. She walked out of the bedroom and I heard her scream. I ran to help, and saw two armed robbers had forced this door open and were invading the house."

"Bastards," the Taser-carrying man said with feeling, staring at the splintered frame. Steyn noted that his hands had relaxed.

"All I could think of was drawing those guns away from Susan and keeping her safe. I shouted to her to run to the bathroom and lock the door. I have some karate experience—in my twenties, I got to brown belt. I was able to tackle one of the men at the door. I knocked his gun out of his hand, and it fell onto the grass outside. Then I kicked him in the groin, so he was out of the fight. But the other aimed his pistol straight at me. It was...I don't know how to describe it. It was like everything happened in slow motion. I flung myself on the ground as he fired twice. The shots went through that window. If I'd been any slower, they would have hit me in the chest."

"Hell. Someone was looking after you there."

"Yes, somebody was. Because after that, I was lying on the ground looking up at the man, and he pointed the gun down at me. He aimed it straight at my head."

"Serious?"

Steyn paused before continuing. "It was a misfire. The gun jammed. But it broke his nerve. The other robber had crawled outside to get his gun, and I think he gave us up as a bad job. He hadn't expected a fight. He ran out, helped his accomplice into the car, and they sped off in that direction." Steyn pointed. Mr. Taser's eyes followed his finger. "The car was a black Toyota," he added.

"Did you get the license plate?"

"I didn't get the plate. But I could identify the guys in a heartbeat if they're found."

Enough with the garrulousness, Steyn decided. A man in shock would either stay silent or babble. He'd babbled enough…it was time to end the story now.

"Man, you had a lucky escape there."

Steyn nodded.

"Have you called the police?"

"We'll go to the police station and report it. I'm not waiting here."

"Can't say I blame you."

"Be careful. They may be in the area, planning to come back. I think you should stay inside, and lock up tight."

Mr. Taser considered this advice before nodding decisively. "I will do. I'm sorry this happened to you."

He turned away and walked down the road. Steyn noted that his tumbledown home was behind a solid, if peeling, wall and had no direct view of this house. All the better. He didn't have to playact any longer. He could get back to work now, and make up for the time he'd lost in spinning that ridiculous story.

Heading toward the highway, Steyn focused on his biggest imperatives.

It was clear where the woman was headed—he'd known

that even before opening her notebook, where the coordinates were written on the very first page. So, imperative number one was to delay the approaching freight truck so that it never reached the rendezvous point. That would mean putting the emergency plan into operation—the one he'd discussed with his employer a while ago.

Imperative number two: he was going to find out who Isobel Collins's knight in shining armor was. It would be easy enough to do, because he'd seen the SUV's license plate during the chase, and he could obtain the owner's name from one of his connections. The SUV driver was posing a serious threat to the success of this job, and he would need to be neutralized. The sooner, the better, because there was a big risk that Isobel would already have told him what she knew.

Steyn adjusted his grip on the steering wheel, noting with surprise that his palms were sweating.

Every job came with unexpected twists. But this one was spiraling out of control, with more and more variables and delays.

Each variable, every delay, meant a massive increase in risk. Covering one set of tracks was easy. But he had left multiple tracks so far, crisscrossing each other, all leading, ultimately, back to him.

Dark places...cramped and airless. The thought of being arrested and locked away made him feel dizzy. He'd never spent a night in prison, but he had older memories of confinement—ones that he couldn't remember clearly, fragments of being somewhere dark, with the only light shining in through a tiny crack above his head, while his heels drummed at the sides of the cupboard, cellar, box…wherever it was that he had been imprisoned. He remembered pain, thirst, gnawing hunger.

Those were the only times he'd ever felt fear.

Steyn reached the highway and put his foot down. After the storm, the evening was cool, and the car's air-conditioning was on its lowest setting. Even so, he felt beads of sweat breaking out on his forehead.

He'd always known, deep down, that one of the jobs he took on would end up being his last.

"But not this one," he muttered, accelerating into the misty evening. "Not this one."

CHAPTER 18

"ARE WE STUCK? We can get through this—can't we?" Isobel looked anxiously at Joey.

Joey took his foot off the gas. Buried in the sticky mud, the uselessly spinning wheels were only digging the SUV deeper. Telling himself not to panic, he looked at the clock, and as he did so, the display changed from 5:39 to 5:40 p.m.

"We may be temporarily stuck, but we'll get out of this," he reassured Isobel.

He opened the door, pushing tufts of wet grass aside, and squelched into the mire.

There was no way around. The mud was caused by a stream that flowed through a deep channel. This was the only crossing point. Usually the stream was no more than a trickle, but the heavy rain had changed that. So, somehow he needed to gain enough traction to get his SUV through the worst of the bog.

What to do?

His strengths lay in creative problem-solving. He'd had a

reputation for being able to achieve the impossible on short notice, back in his corporate days. Now he needed to draw on his reserves of resourcefulness and wile.

He scanned the area. A few yards farther on were some splintered planks. He guessed that at some time past, somebody had tried to use them to cross the mud, but they hadn't been long enough. They certainly wouldn't be long enough to cover the mud now, but he could think of another way of using them.

He thought again about the inventory of essentials in the trunk of his car. A change of clothes, cable ties, duct tape, a knife, and rope—generous supplies of all of them. In this situation, duct tape would be the most useful.

"What are we doing?"

He turned to see Isobel standing behind him. The mud was oozing over her smart white sneakers, but it didn't seem to bother her.

"We're going to turn the car into a tank," he told her.

"How're we going to do that?"

Joey walked over to the planks and selected two pieces, each a little over two feet long, and a few inches wide.

"We're going to fasten these to the tires. That way, when the wheels turn, the planks will create more surface area and bite into the mud, just as if they were the tracks on a tank. Here, you hold the plank on top of the front wheel. I'm going to tape it into place, and then we'll do the other side."

Joey fastened the plank to the top of the tire using the duct tape, winding it round and round, before wading to the other side. The mire was deeper here, so he used the longer plank. By that stage his fingers were covered in mud, making it difficult to wrap the tape properly.

"Let me do it." Isobel, whose hands were drier, took over and efficiently unrolled the tape over the plank, and through the gap in the wheel.

"Thanks," Joey said. "Great job."

"Hey, no worries. It's great to feel useful. Makes a change."

She smiled at him. She had dirt smudged across her cheek, and he wanted to touch her face, to wipe it gently away.

A change from what? he wondered, deciding not to ask.

Instead, he grinned back. "Well, now for the important part—let's see if it works." Squelching over to the trunk, he found an old towel to clean their hands with. Nothing short of a pressure hose was going to shift the stuff layered over their shoes and ankles.

When Joey, Isobel, and a fair amount of the mud were back in the car, he started it up again and eased forward. The wheels spun…and then the planks bit in. With a heavy lurch, the car jerked forward. When the planks left the ground, the wheels continued spinning, but when the wood came round again, they made another jump forward.

"Slowly does it," he encouraged the SUV.

"I hope the tape holds." Isobel leaned out of the window, anxiously surveying her handiwork.

"It should."

Carefully, Joey inched the car through the most treacherous section. There was something deeply satisfying about feeling the wooden planks dig into the ground, defying the drag and suck of the mud and propelling the car forward, even if only a short distance at a time.

Gradually, the SUV's wheels gained purchase, and its momentum increased, powering steadily up the hill. He drove for another minute before he risked stopping.

Then he breathed a sigh of relief, because they'd done it.

"Excellent work." He and Isobel exchanged a grimy high-five before Joey climbed out and quickly removed the planks.

Checking his phone, he saw he had three bars of signal. More than enough to lead them to Isobel's coordinates that, according to the map, were four minutes away. They should be in time.

He guessed that if her husband's business was road freighting, the coordinates would lead to a depot, or rendezvous point of some kind near a highway. However, they were definitely more than four minutes away from any of the main roads.

"Carry on with what you were saying," he encouraged Isobel. "The background. You need to brief me before we arrive at wherever we're going."

"After the bombshell of what Samantha told me, I became an investigator, together with her, as we tried to work out what was going on. It was a massive task. First, we had to gather all the puzzle pieces. Then we had to put them in order, analyzing the information we'd obtained. Vehicle numbers, times, load weights, drivers, routes. It felt like I was actually using my brain for the first time in years." She laughed.

"And why did these coordinates come up?"

"Because we worked out that the truck driving this route always makes unscheduled stops at that point, for two or three hours at a time. Usually, the loads are lighter after the stop, when the truck is driving south. But occasionally, going north, they're heavier again."

Joey nodded, wondering what the reason was for this. Smuggling goods into Johannesburg? But then why the heavier loads going north?

"Also, we discovered there's only one driver who does this route. All the other drivers get switched between routes and shifts so that the trucks run full time. But not this one. He drives his route back and forth, back and forth, doing trips every two weeks, and the rest of the time the truck stands idle. The route goes from Zambia in the north, down through Zimbabwe, through eastern Johannesburg and into the city center, before heading back again."

"Any idea what the truck brings down?"

"Coffee loads are quite common. The beans come from a co-op in the north of Zambia, but the rest of the time the cargo varies. Wood, maize, tobacco. All from different suppliers. But no matter what goods are transported, there's the same discrepancy in the weights every two or three trips."

"And your husband didn't pick this up?" Joey asked incredulously.

"The stats weren't easy to interpret," she said. "We had to do a lot of research."

"Did you try showing him the evidence?"

Isobel made a face. "Yes, I tried, but he wouldn't hear me out. He said I was wrong, and that my calculations were incorrect. He said the weight disparities were normal, and that Brogan had told him they were due to the truck's fuel consumption because, on this route, they loaded several containers of diesel in Zambia and used it along the way."

Joey kept quiet, deciding it wouldn't be prudent to offer his opinion on Dave's response. This told him something about their marriage, though. It was clear that Isobel didn't have a voice. Not one that her husband listened to, anyway.

"And Dave didn't explain why the business was bleeding profits, either," Isobel added sadly. "So Samantha and I discussed it, and I decided I was going to travel out here to see for myself. I sent her the details of my flights and where I was staying, in case anything went wrong, but she promised me she wouldn't say a word to anyone."

"And you're sure you trust Samantha?" Joey asked, thinking about the hitman who'd come so close to killing Isobel.

"Oh, yes, I trust her totally," Isobel said.

"People can sometimes give information away innocently," Joey warned her, keeping his voice gentle. "Especially if they have no reason to be distrustful."

Now, looking at Isobel again, he saw the beginnings of doubt in her eyes.

CHAPTER 19

FIVE MINUTES TO six, and Steyn's tracking system, now back online, informed him that the truck was running twenty minutes late. Another truck had jackknifed in the storm, which in turn had caused heavy traffic delays north of Pretoria.

That meant his next job was a particularly ugly one, and something he had not been looking forward to, for a variety of reasons. Firstly, there was little skill involved in its execution; it was a task even a pig-ignorant muscle man could have done. And secondly, it involved going underground, which was not something Steyn would have willingly chosen.

However, he was a professional, and this was merely another chore to perform, part of an assignment for which he was receiving an extremely high payment.

He drove off the highway, along a tar road that turned to dirt a few kilometers later. At the end of the dirt road was a large ROAD CLOSED barrier, with faded yellow chevrons. However, somebody arriving at the barrier who took a closer look would see the signs of flattened grass where cars had driven around the sign, just as Steyn was doing now.

A little farther along the road, which was now little more than a bumpy track, was another weathered sign. EGOLI EAST RAND GOLD MINE. ENTRANCE CLOSED. ACCESS PROHIBITED BY LAW.

And, beyond that, Steyn noticed a third sign. This one was newer, but it had been pulled off its post and now lay, faceup, on the ground nearby.

PREMISES SECURED BY PRIVATE JOHANNESBURG.

At that moment, Steyn's phone beeped. He had an incoming message—information on the SUV's license plate, which he had requested earlier.

He read the message.

Then he looked down again at the sign on the ground.

His thin lips hooked into another joyless smile. Coincidence sometimes worked in strange ways.

Steyn parked the BMW behind a row of bushes farther on, so it was not visible from the road.

He ducked under the chain-link fence outside the mine's entrance, which displayed another CLOSED—WARNING—DANGER notice, rattling in the breeze.

Beyond that was the entrance, a square tunnel blasted in the rock. The solid wooden boards that had been nailed over the entrance to block access were now ripped away. Most of them had already been cut up and used for firewood. A few splintered pieces still lay nearby. Walking through the entrance, he breathed in the chilly, stale-smelling air and his skin prickled automatically into gooseflesh.

The tunnel sloped gradually down into darkness, and Steyn had to switch on his phone's flashlight. At the end of the tunnel was a shaft, where a rickety ladder had been placed to allow access to the deep.

Steyn realized he was breathing much faster than he should have after the short walk. He was imagining the tons of rock pressing down on him. His flashlight beam bobbed over the heaps of crushed ore lining the passage. In some of them, he could see gold flecks gleaming.

From far below, he could hear the clanging of tools and the far-off sound of voices as the workers—a team of zama zamas—chipped away at the reef.

He lowered a thick plastic hose a few feet down the shaft. It was attached to a large machine. The zama zamas were used to the humming sound as the pump started up, removing the dusty air and replacing it with fresh air from the surface. Up until now, it had been used only for that purpose.

This time, Steyn attached the hose to a different side of the machine.

Now, when the pump started working, it would flood the chamber below with deadly carbon monoxide. In an hour, all fifty of the workers below would be dead.

The rattle of the pump muffled the sound of Steyn pulling up the ladder, so that they would have no way out.

After covering and locking the machine's ignition switch,

he loosened a rope that held a heavy steel grating against the wall. He moved the hose into a niche in the rock, because when this grating came down, it wasn't going up again...it weighed close to half a ton.

He pulled on the rope, hearing the grinding as it loosened and began to topple forward.

He stepped back and squeezed his eyes shut as it crashed down, sending dust and rock fragments billowing into the air.

A few seconds later, he opened his eyes again, and blinked the residue of dust away.

The hose was undamaged, safe in its niche.

The grating was immovably in place.

He could hear a few concerned shouts coming from below. Well, there was nothing they could do now. The underground chamber, together with their fate, was sealed.

Steyn hurried up the passage as he heard the zama zamas' screams begin. He had expected that he would be pleased and relieved that this part of the job was done, and he would never have to come back here again.

But somewhere deep inside, he was screaming, too.

CHAPTER 20

JOEY AND ISOBEL arrived at the coordinates exactly as the car clock flashed over to 6:01.

"Is this the right place?" Isobel asked uncertainly. The headlights cut the gathering darkness, showing that they were stopped on a large, barren piece of ground between the dirt track they'd been traveling on and a sand road that Joey guessed would eventually lead to the highway some distance away.

There was nobody else there. The rain had stopped, leaving the evening cool and clear. The setting sun was buried in a mass of clouds, and the first stars were shining overhead. Joey heard crickets chirping nearby and, from somewhere in the distance, the sound of frogs.

"This is definitely correct," Joey said. "I guess it's a rendezvous point, for who knows what. Out of the way, and leading to nothing but an abandoned site."

"Do you think we're too late?" Isobel gazed at the darkening landscape surrounding them.

"What time did the records state the trucks arrived?"

"Most often at six precisely—occasionally a minute or two later. They stopped for about a quarter of an hour, and then left again."

Joey wondered what that implied. Probably a swift transfer of goods, done in the shortest possible time frame. Although six p.m. always made him think of shift changes, of guards coming and going from their posts on site.

"The storm might have caused delays. Let's wait a few minutes and see what happens," he said. On this flat piece of land, they'd be able to spot an oncoming vehicle from far away. But the driver would be able to see them, too. Joey decided it would be better to find cover. He wanted to be very careful, especially since the gunman who'd followed them earlier might not have given up. The chances were slim that the man knew where the back roads led, but Joey wasn't going to risk getting in his sights a second time.

He drove in a large circle, looking carefully at the surrounding landscape. There was little in the way of shelter, but he saw some small trees in the distance behind a ROAD CLOSED sign.

"Shall we park behind those bushes?" Isobel was obviously thinking the same way he was.

"If we can get there."

Driving closer, he saw there was a gap next to the sign. In fact, it looked as if somebody had driven through it very recently. There were fresh tire tracks in the muddy ground. Isobel saw them, too, and tensed.

"You think someone's there?"

"I can see two sets of tracks. More likely a car came and went." All the same, he put a hand on his holstered pistol, checking that he'd be able to draw it quickly if he needed to.

"Is there anything down this road?"

"It leads to a closed mine shaft, part of the Egoli East mine. It's one of the places I worked with, although we accessed the site from the main entrance on the other side of the mine, where the roads are better." Carefully, Joey drove round the sign before stopping.

"Why was it closed?"

"It became too dangerous to mine from the current access points. The rock above the reef is weak and riddled with fault lines. There were three tunnel collapses, each resulting in miners being trapped underground for days. They were lucky there were no fatalities. So they decided to close it until a safer tunnel could be constructed."

"Do you think it's being mined illegally?"

"I do. Unfortunately a lot of people know how rich it is, so it's an obvious target. When Private Johannesburg had the contract, we posted two guards on duty here at all times. They patrolled the whole area, guarding the main and side entrances, which were both sealed."

He looked at his watch, then down at the tracks again. "It's ten past six now. We're outside your rendezvous time frame."

"So we missed our chance. That gunman must have known where we were heading and warned them not to come." Isobel's voice was heavy with disappointment.

"These tire tracks might provide another clue, or at least a chance to find new information. If they continue all the way to the mine's entrance, that tells us something. We can check whether the access is still sealed, or if someone has tried to break in."

He stopped the SUV behind the trees and killed the lights. Treading carefully in the near-darkness, they set off along the path.

CHAPTER 21

JOEY AND ISOBEL approached the mine entrance—the concrete building that marked it was no more than a black outline against the darkening sky. In the quietness of the evening, the scrunch of their feet over the gravel path sounded very loud. Joey's instincts were prickling. "I think we're headed for trouble," he told Isobel.

"I'm worried," she said softly.

He wanted to take her hand, or to put his arm around her; to offer her physical comfort and security. But that wouldn't be right, he decided. Better to support her with words alone.

"We're only going to look," he said, glancing down at a sandy channel where he could see the faint indentations of footprints. "If we see anything wrong, we call the police."

"I agree we should do that, but that's not why I'm worried. I think…well, it's a big coincidence that my coordinates brought us here. Why do the truck stops all occur so close to this supposedly closed mine? What if Brogan's involved in this illegal mining, and he's transporting the gold?"

"It would suggest a connection. But, logically, if a transport truck was collecting large quantities of ore from the mine, it would be heavier after leaving, not lighter. And if they were processing the gold on site, then the weight difference would be negligible, since it takes tons of ore to create only a few ounces of gold. But even so, let's not rule it out, if you suspect it. You have good instincts." In fact, Joey realized, in the short time they'd known each other, he had developed the utmost respect for Isobel's guts, her judgment, and her intelligence. It bothered him that her husband didn't seem to appreciate these qualities as much as he should.

Then he stopped dead, taking Isobel by the arm. Her skin felt warm and, to his surprise, she grasped his arm in turn.

"What is it?" she breathed.

"It's broken open." Joey stared at the concrete building that marked the start of the tunnel. The boards that sealed its entrance had been ripped away, and the door beyond was forced wide.

The zama zamas were back.

CHAPTER 22

"YOU THINK THE zama zamas are actually inside?" Isobel whispered, staring at the pitch-black gap leading to the tunnel. She was glad that Joey was beside her. She found he reassured her in a way that went beyond the presence of his muscular and imposing body. He was calm, capable, surprisingly sensitive to her needs, and shrewdly intelligent.

"It's very likely they may be here," he replied. "We may be able to hear some activity if we go in, but first, let's call for backup."

"Who are you going to call?"

"First, the cops. Secondly, an ambulance."

"Ambulance?"

"Confrontations between police and zama zamas tend to end violently."

Isobel waited, watching, while Joey made the calls.

No sign of any vehicle approaching. She was sure now that the truck driver had been warned to avoid the meeting point. If that was so, then perhaps Joey was right, and the evidence they had discovered—the tire tracks and the breached mine entrance—would explain these specially scheduled detours. That would mean her husband's South African employees had become involved in illegal mining.

Her thoughts were in turmoil as she considered how they might have found out she was here. Had Samantha innocently said something to the wrong person?

But then something else caught her attention. It was a strange, faraway sound, only just audible in the quiet of the night.

At first, she thought it might be an approaching truck; it was a low, drumming noise that reminded her of tires over rough ground, only not quite the same.

She turned toward the direction of the road to try to hear it better, but when she did, it faded away.

She moved closer to the concrete entrance, and that was when she heard it again.

Curious, she stepped through the dark mouth of the gateway, and then walked a few more steps. Now the throbbing was resonating through her body, the booming sound punctuated by sharper cracks, and a low babble of what might be voices. Shivers chilled the length of her spine and she felt her neck prickle.

"Joey," she called.

He was off his phone, and he must have instantly picked up on her fear. In a few giant strides, he was inside.

"What's wrong?"

"Listen."

Joey listened, then spoke again, sounding shaken. "I don't know what the hell's going on down below, but something is seriously wrong."

"Why?" Her mouth felt suddenly dry.

"Those aren't the sounds of mining. They're drumming on the rock with tools. I think trying to call for help, but it could also cause a structural collapse. People must be trapped down there." He stared down the pitch-black tunnel. "We have to get them out."

CHAPTER 23

SHADRACK MASHISHI WAS driving to the drop-off point as fast as he could. He was behind schedule and in a panic about it, because it wasn't good to arrive late when working for these bosses.

It was only his job to drive. That was why he had a job. Because he drove capably, and because he was prepared to do what he was told without asking questions. He knew he was lucky to have work at all with his criminal record—a six-month conviction for assault and battery after a vicious bar fight some years ago.

At first, he thought the silver BMW coming up behind him was a hijacker because of the speed with which it approached, flashing its lights as it stormed along in his lane. Then the car passed, and Shadrack was just heaving a sigh of relief when the brake lights flashed and it swerved in again.

"Shit!" Clamping his jaw tight, he slammed on the brakes, feeling the truck start to fishtail on the wet road. He prayed it wouldn't overturn and cause him to lose the official load of coffee beans that he'd freighted from Zambia. As for the un-official load, hidden behind an inner panel—well, he was sure the twenty men crammed in there would have a few bruises after his evasive maneuver.

He skidded to a stop behind the BMW. After a moment to collect himself, it occurred to Shadrack that this might be one of his employers. Maybe plans had changed. Either way, he needed to stay calm. A tall, thin man unfolded himself from the car and strode over, grinning at him with a lopsided smile that stretched only as far as his cheekbones, leaving his eyes stony cold.

"Shadrack?"

Definitely one of the boss men.

"Yes," he replied, opening the door and climbing down. He focused on trying to appear willing, not letting his face show the mixture of exhaustion and fear that was seething inside him.

"This is a precautionary stop. There's a situation to resolve at the site, so we are delaying delivery of the cargo."

"Ah," Shadrack said. He wondered how long the wait would be. He had his own deadlines to meet. When border officials were routinely bribed so that a search meant open-ing the truck's back door and glancing inside—well, a man ended up doing favors for friends. And branching out into additional enterprises to cover expenses. There were some pills stashed in the door compartment, and a couple of underage pornographic DVDs he'd obtained to sell on. That particular market wasn't his taste, but it sure paid well for material.

"Did you know the rear-access door of your truck is loose?" the cold-eyed man asked him, and something in his tone made Shadrack's stomach lurch. "You could be fired for that. Get round the back, check your cargo, and close it properly."

"Will do." Shadrack pulled himself up straighter. Suddenly it was like this guy had planted a ramrod in his spine. He marched round to the back of the truck and stepped up to the small access door.

Loose? It didn't look loose. Still, it wouldn't hurt to make sure. Go through the motions, please the people who signed the paychecks.

He opened the door, looked obediently in at the closely stacked sacks, and closed it again, twisting the handle vigorously.

When he looked back at the man, a gun had materialized in his hand, its cold black eye staring directly into Shadrack's own.

"Hey," he shouted. "Wait!"

Shadrack wanted to run, but bright headlights filled his vision, an approaching truck was blinding him, and the hard-eyed man paused, as if waiting for the truck to pass before doing the deed.

Then darkness swallowed him.

CHAPTER 24

JOEY AND ISOBEL raced down the tunnel. Joey's flashlight shone on the walls, glimmering off the shards of minerals trapped in the dark bedrock and the piles of ore stored along the tunnel's sides.

As they ran, the noise increased, becoming a pandemonium.

The clanging of tools, the scream of metal on rock. The desperate cries of men coming from deeper underground, although there were too many voices to make out the words.

"What's happening?"

"A rock fall, a gas leak, a flood…" Scenarios spun through Joey's head as he sprinted to the tunnel's end, keeping his head down to avoid the low, rough ceiling. Here was the shaft, but there was a grate over it—a massive structure that must weigh half a ton. And below the grate, somebody had run a pipe through a gap in the rock. Gas was hissing through it, coming from a large machine that was rattling nearby.

"Air!" Now he could hear some of the cries clearly. "Help us! Air!"

"They can't get out," Isobel said, her voice filled with horror. "They're trapped down there. How can we lift the grate?"

Moving it with manpower alone would be impossible for two people; this was a job for ten. But Joey realized there was a more serious issue.

"What's going through that pipe?" Leaning forward, Joey examined the machine. If the miners' escape route had been deliberately blocked, it was likely that these fumes were toxic. Somebody was making sure these men would not get out alive.

"We're here to help you!" he shouted down.

In answer came more desperate cries. "Air, please! Air."

Something as basic as carbon monoxide from a simple gasoline engine would swiftly be lethal in the confined space where the zama zamas worked, and this looked like a gasoline engine to him.

"Stop shouting!" he yelled to the men below. "Save your breath—breathe slowly, stand still. I'm going to try and get you out of here."

He thought they'd heard and understood, because gradually, the shouting and banging subsided.

First step—turn this damn thing off.

"Where the hell is the ignition switch?" he muttered.

"Here?" Isobel pointed to a steel panel. "Perhaps it's behind this."

"It's been locked." Joey's heart sank. The panel looked to be a homemade addition, simple but effective. It had been welded onto the engine, and the switch was indeed behind it.

"If we can't turn it off, let's pull it up. That should buy them a little more time. At least they won't be getting directly flooded by it."

"Good idea."

With his heart pounding hard, Joey pulled up the hose, working as fast as he could. The pipe felt warm to the touch, throbbing as the fumes pulsed through it. Drawing it through the narrow gap was a difficult job, and he was aware of the seconds ticking inexorably by as more contaminated air gathered in the space below. Sweat trickled down his temples and he shook it away.

Finally, it was up. He grabbed the end of the hose and ran with it, back toward the entrance, dropping it as far from the grate as he could. It didn't stretch very far, but at least now the fumes were not being channeled directly into the rocky chamber.

Of course, the downside was that the fumes were now spewing into the badly ventilated passage where Joey and Isobel needed to work.

"How much time do we have?" Isobel sounded anxious.

"A few minutes, I hope." Joey coughed as the petrol fumes caught in his throat. In the precious time that remained, they had to figure out how to lift the heavy grate, so that they could free the zama zamas.

Joey shone the flashlight round, looking for anything that could help. A ladder lay nearby that must have been pulled up before the grate was lowered. So where had the grate been before that?

On the opposite wall was a thick steel hook that must have held it up. But now it was lowered, there was no way of lifting it again, and nothing to secure it with.

He had rope in his car, though…lots of it.

Joey was starting to feel dizzy and light-headed. His head was pounding.

"Outside," he gasped.

The clean night air poured into his lungs, flooding him with oxygen again. Beside him, he saw Isobel breathing deeply, but her face was drawn.

"How are we going to move that grate?"

Out here in the fresh night air, his head felt suddenly clearer.

"We can use the rope and the hook. Create a pulley system."

"Using the car!" Isobel completed his thought. "Run the rope from the grating, up through the hook, then out to the car's tow hitch. Drive the car forward, and it will lift the grating up to the hook."

"It could just work."

"It has to work," she replied.

CHAPTER 25

JOEY RACED TO his SUV. He climbed in, and reversed it as close as he could to the tunnel's entrance. How much rope did he have? Would it be enough?

He opened the trunk and pulled out the nylon coils. Now, as he thought about the massive weight of the grate, the rope seemed flimsy and he was seriously worried it wouldn't be long enough. But all they could do was try...there was no other hope for the men below.

"Let's tie the rope to the grate first, and then string it back to the car," he said. "We don't want to be fiddling around in there longer than we have to."

"Breathe deeply now, before we go in," Isobel advised, and they spent a few seconds drawing long breaths before jogging down the darkened passageway. The fumes stung his eyes; he wished for the storm to return, forcing air into this tunnel, but the breeze had dropped and the night was still.

Isobel shone the flashlight onto the grate, and Joey tied a bowline knot. His fingers felt clumsy—he supposed either from haste or the insidious effect of the gas. The hook was a few inches above his outstretched arms, but he propped the ladder against the wall and stood on the second rung. Hastily, he fed the rope through the hook.

"Out," he said, after pushing the ladder clear, and they ran back to the entrance, Joey holding tight to the coiled loops, paying them out as he went, aware with a sick certainty that the rope was slipping through his hands too fast.

He was dizzy, leadenness spreading in his limbs and nausea churning in the pit of his belly. He was worried that the zama zamas weren't keeping quiet because he'd asked them to, but because they had succumbed to the flood of poisoned air.

"It's too short!" Despair crushed him. They were standing just one pace away from his car, and he'd run out of rope. He pulled as hard as he could on the remaining length, staring in despair at the short, but insurmountable, distance between the end of the nylon line and his tow hitch.

There was no way he could drive in any farther. The tunnel was a few inches narrower than his car, and the back of the vehicle was already almost flush with the rock.

"Your cable ties! I saw them in there earlier. Surely we could use them to make up the distance?" Isobel rummaged in the open trunk and pulled out a handful of them.

"That could work. Their breaking strength, though…"

"What is the strength?"

"About two hundred pounds per tie."

"And if you use more than one?"

"Then it multiplies the strength."

"How much does the grate weigh?"

"That's the million-dollar question," Joey acknowledged.

He had no idea what its weight would be, but he guessed at least half a ton. So, to be safe and create a margin for error, he needed seven ties per loop. How many loops would he need to cover the distance? And how many cable ties did he have? He found two more packets in the back of his car. He passed one to Isobel and they tore them open. Joey's bag ripped down the side and the black ties scattered over the ground.

Isobel was neater-fingered than he was, and worked faster. In a few minutes, while Joey was still struggling with his fourth link, she had made six tidy bundles.

The only problem was they were starting to run short of cable ties. Joey shone his flashlight over the ground, brushing it with his fingers, hoping to pick up any of the ones that had fallen. Isobel was creating another link, looping the two lengths they'd made together.

"I'm two ties short here," she said. "Are there any others?"

"I can't find any." Joey swept the area with his flashlight and fingers again, wishing for his fingertips to touch one of those precious pieces of plastic, but they didn't. There were no more.

One link would have to have only five ties in it.

Joey looped the end of the chain around the tow hitch. There was just enough rope for him to tie a secure knot on the other end.

"Now we see if it works," he said. He didn't have a clue if it would. He was having serious doubts about the sanity of using a few pieces of plastic, underspecified for the job, to try to hold up a deadly weight long enough for them to rescue everyone trapped inside.

But it was their only chance.

"I'm going to get into the car now and ease it forward," he told her. "I'll do it as slowly as possible, so as not to put more strain on the cables. Take the flashlight and shine it down the passage. Tell me if it's working, and if the grate is lifting."

"Will do," Isobel confirmed.

Joey would rather have had her behind the wheel and himself exposed to further fumes in the passage, but it was better for the person more familiar with the car to do the job. And he would prefer for the burden of failure to fall on his own shoulders than on hers.

"Easy now," he urged the big SUV, as he disengaged the hand brake and pressed down on the gas pedal. He could visualize the rows of looped plastic tautening, taking strain as the rope tightened. He imagined the weight of the grate. God, what if they'd been totally wrong in judging it? He was bracing himself for the sudden lurch forward that would mean one of the links had broken.

Instead, the SUV eased a foot forward, then another, and he heard Isobel shout: "It's lifting!"

Carefully, carefully...it would be so easy to overshoot, to draw this contraption of plastic and rope beyond its breaking point. Perhaps another foot. He edged the car forward, imagining the steel grate lifting, its full weight bearing down as it rose.

"Go higher!" Isobel called, her voice sounding hoarse.

Joey eased forward another foot, and then another, and when he heard her cry of "Stop!" he reacted immediately, cranking the hand brake as tight as it would go and hoping it would hold. He left the car in gear, turned it off, and then he was out and racing back down the tunnel.

The grate was open, angled over the gap and making him think of a jaw waiting to snap shut. But, so far, it was holding.

CHAPTER 26

"YOU STAY OUTSIDE," Joey urged Isobel. His face looked drawn from strain.

"But you'll need help," she protested, as he lowered the ladder down.

"I don't know how strong the fumes are down there. One of us needs to stay out, to deal with the emergency services when they arrive."

"Okay," she agreed reluctantly, feeling her heart clench with worry as he clambered down. She could hear a few faint cries coming from below, but she feared that he was right, and that many of the miners had already succumbed to the fumes.

"Keep away from the grate," Joey warned. Then he disappeared into the smoky darkness.

Isobel glanced up at the grate, noticing the jagged metal along its edge, speckled with rust. She stepped hurriedly back, imagining it slamming down. What could she do? She thought she could hear Joey's voice coming from far below, speaking gently.

She prayed the emergency services would come soon. With their supplies of oxygen and other equipment, the rescue might stand a chance. She ran down the tunnel and out into the night.

She thought she could see them, far away in the distance—a faint patterning of red lights cutting the humid air. It would take another few minutes for them to get close enough to see her.

Something crunched under her feet, and she bent to pick it up.

It was a cable tie.

But, when she looked at it more closely, she realized it wasn't an unused one.

This tie had stretched and snapped, right next to its fastening. Horror flooded through her as she saw it. One had broken, stressed to its limits, creating a weakness that would allow more to follow.

Adrenaline surging through her, Isobel screamed, "Joey! Hurry!"

That single snapped tie meant that there might be only a few minutes left. Maybe less. She needed to buy more time…

The car jack!

It could prove useful now to keep that lethal wedge of metal suspended and prevent it crashing down again.

She grabbed the jack and sprinted down the tunnel. The wave of dizziness she felt from the fumes almost knocked her off her feet, but she struggled forward. Where, and how, to position it? If she wedged it as close as possible to the base of the grate, and then cranked it upward, that would create an additional support, and hopefully take some of the strain off the makeshift rope.

Fingers shaking with tension, Isobel cranked up the jack. One turn, two…It was holding now, and seemed to be wedged firmly enough in place that it wouldn't shift. Hopefully, with this to support the grate, the rope would hold for long enough to get the miners out.

She could hear the sirens in the distance.

Running back to the entrance, hoping the gunman was not waiting and watching somewhere, Isobel headed out into the night.

"Here! Quick!" she screamed and waved her arms.

The sound of the sirens grew louder and headlights blazed in her eyes as the first ambulance sped toward her.

CHAPTER 27

SCRAMBLING DOWN THE ladder, Joey descended into a cramped underground hell. The engine fumes were stronger down here. The air was filled with choking fumes, but Joey could also pick up the sour stench of unwashed bodies, and the reek of vomit. Nausea roiled inside him, his body's reaction to the toxic air. He tried to suppress it as hands from below reached up to grasp him, and hoarse voices pleaded for his help. His flashlight shone over their terrified faces and dread stabbed him as he saw a few had already collapsed on the ground.

"Right, come on. Let's get you out of here."

There was a language barrier to overcome; Joey had a basic knowledge of Zulu and Sotho, but some of the men had no English and didn't speak either of these local languages. He had a sense that they were not down here voluntarily. He'd met a few zama zamas during security operations in this area. They had been hard and dangerous men, often with a criminal history, and prone to violence. Perhaps it was the effect of the gas, but these miners appeared only frightened and confused.

As he started organizing a hasty triage system, he clearly heard the sound that he had feared most. A harsh, grinding noise started, and then stopped abruptly. It told him that the grate had started to slip. One of the links must have weakened. If the rope broke entirely, the grate would crash down, an unstoppable weight, sealing the entrance again.

Nothing he could do now…he just had to get these men out as fast as possible.

And then, as he helped the first of the survivors up the ladder, a prolonged, harsh, scraping sound from above made his heart jump into his throat. At first he thought the grate was falling—that they were all doomed.

But as he struggled to the surface with the first of the weakened men, he saw that Isobel had used the car jack, jamming it into the angle of steel and cranking it up so that this sturdy structure took strain off the rope.

Then footsteps were rushing to meet them, flashlights cutting the darkness. The paramedics had arrived. Moments later, the weight of the miner's body was lifted from his arms.

"Oxygen. Quick!" Joey called, and within seconds, life-saving supplies were making their way down the ladder in the hands of two more paramedics. In that instant, Joey knew that the miners' lives were going to be saved.

He wanted to hug Isobel, to take her in his arms and feel the warmth of her against him, to smooth down that spiky blond hair and watch her smile up at him, because they had done it. The two of them together had achieved the impossible in bringing the men to safety.

But when he finally left the tunnel and strode out into the open air, he didn't get that chance.

CHAPTER 28

THE AREA OUTSIDE the mine's entrance was bustling with activity, and lit by flashing red and blue lights. Medics shouted to each other, and police walkie-talkies crackled. Joey saw that the miners were all being given oxygen and were being divided into two groups—those who needed immediate hospitalization, and those who were less severely affected, who were being interviewed by police.

"So you didn't know you were going to be working down a mine?" Joey heard one of the officers ask a raggedly dressed zama zama. The man, who obviously understood some English, shook his head before replying haltingly.

"They told us we would be carrying rocks to the surface. They said that the business would organize us all the proper permits, and that the money would be good. It was only when we came here that we found they had lied to us."

The miner's story confirmed Joey's suspicions—the men had, indeed, been trafficked here. He should tell Isobel. Where was she? Looking around, he found himself smiling when he caught sight of her. She was standing apart from the group and watching the headlights of another approaching car. He called her name, but in the hubbub, she didn't hear. He started walking toward her, feeling suddenly nervous of what else he should say. He still wanted to give her that hug—but should he drive her back into town? Buy her dinner? Help her find better lodgings?

He had a very comfortable spare room in his own house, where Hayley sometimes stayed. He should offer it to her…but he knew that if she came to his home, he wouldn't want her to sleep in the spare room. Thinking this way about her was going to be dangerous at best, depressing at worst.

Driving her to a good hotel with top-class security would be most sensible. He was still concerned about her safety, and guessed she'd have a busy evening updating her husband on the goings-on within his company that he should already have known about. From the sounds of things, Dave had been neglecting his business—and his wife.

But could this have been done deliberately?

Once the suspicion had lodged itself in Joey's mind, it refused to leave. He decided that after he'd dropped Isobel at her hotel, he was going to call Jack Morgan, brief him on the situation and ask for his opinion, because something about it didn't feel right.

Abruptly, the approaching headlights swung in Isobel's direction. A moment later, the car stopped, and a tall man climbed out. Joey saw Isobel's posture instantly freeze into shock, and for one horrified moment, he thought the gunman had arrived.

He was already sprinting forward and fumbling for his gun when he saw her demeanor relax. The tall man opened his arms as Isobel shook her head, and he thought he heard the sound of her laughter. Then they embraced and Joey slowed his pace.

"Dave!" he heard her say. "What on earth are you doing here? How did you even know I was in South Africa?"

"Samantha called me yesterday," the American explained. Joey noted he was blond, well built, with strong, handsome features. "Samantha discovered that Brogan had intercepted some of the e-mails you girls sent to each other."

You girls? Joey wanted to grab the man by his broad shoulders and shake him hard.

"Brogan intercepted them?" Isobel asked.

"Yes. Samantha was worried when you messaged that your bodyguard had been canceled. She got an IT specialist in who confirmed that the e-mail server had been reconfigured to forward all correspondence between you two to Brogan at the South African office. She contacted me immediately. I was in Cape Town, waiting to catch a flight back to the States, so I got on a plane and flew straight up here instead."

"I had no idea you knew!" Isobel cried.

"No, *I* had no idea you were doing this. Why didn't you tell me?"

"Well, I tried to, but…"

"Next time, you tell me about these things. You've done an amazing job here, baby girl, but seriously, you were in massive danger. I'm not gonna let you out of the house when we get home. I nearly had a heart attack when I heard about this crazy scheme."

"But you're not…"

"Come on. Let's get out of this dump and go somewhere civilized. I've called the police already and they're on the way to arrest Brogan. I've got a room booked for us tonight at the Michelangelo Hotel, Sandton, and we'll fly back home in the morning."

"My luggage!" Isobel exclaimed. "I left my bags in the rental lodgings."

Dave frowned impatiently. "It's late already, baby girl. We'll pick up what you need in the mall next to the hotel, and my PA can organize for the bags to be couriered back home."

Perhaps it was the residual effect of the toxic fumes, but Joey felt suddenly nauseated. He turned away. No point in staying here…there was nothing more he could do. The trafficked miners had been rescued, and Isobel was booked into a secure hotel, where she would be safe until her departure. He'd call her sometime, and tell her good-bye.

Maybe tomorrow.

Maybe never.

CHAPTER 29

LOCK-PICKING WAS an acquired art, and Steyn had made himself proficient at it. There was a time and a place for forcing a door. Because it was noisy, you gained the element of fear, which could be very useful depending on who the victim was, but you sacrificed the element of surprise. In this case, surprise was more important, because his target owned a firearm, which was usually kept in the safe.

Steyn did not want to give him enough time to access the safe.

After waiting until the security guard who patrolled this neighborhood had turned the corner, Steyn came out of hiding and quickly climbed the wall. Then he walked through the well-kept garden, breathing in the fresh scent of flowers and leaves still wet from the rain. He did some work on the house alarm's electronics box before making his way to the imposing wooden front door. The target lived well in this rental accommodation—Steyn guessed that African network manager was a very senior position. Clearly Brogan also felt safe in these lodgings because the alarm had not, in fact, been turned on.

A minute's stealthy work at the front door, and Steyn was inside, his soft shoes padding across the marble hallway. A trickle of sweat inched down his forehead, surprising him with its presence. It wasn't such a warm night. But then, he was operating on a knife edge right now, riding out the rodeo that this job had become, leaving him far from his usual state of implacable calm.

The television blared from the living room on the right. He listened for voices—there were none to be heard. Brogan lived alone, but occasionally brought women home for the night. Steyn guessed this was not one of those nights. He hadn't thought it would be. Even though he had every reason to want to relieve his stress, Brogan must have been too preoccupied to visit the trendy nightclub a few blocks away, which was his normal hunting ground.

That meant he'd chosen another way of relieving his inner tensions.

Brogan was a heavy drinker. If he hadn't had time to go down to the club, then without a doubt, he would have opened a bottle from the stash of single malt whiskey in the cellar.

A snore coming from the living room told Steyn he was correct.

The living room was spacious and sumptuous, with white tiling, dark leather furniture, and tasteful modern art on the walls that Steyn was sure Brogan did not appreciate. The man himself was slumped on his back on the couch. A whiskey glass lay on its side nearby, and the room stank like a distillery.

From the television, an episode of *The Jerry Springer Show* blared.

"Brogan?" Steyn asked softly, holding the gun at the ready.

The African network manager didn't respond, but let out a loud, reverberating snore.

Time to do what needed to be done. Having the man unconscious would make it easier. The layout of the house was perfect for Steyn's needs, with those long, exposed rafters running across the length of the living room's ceiling.

He flung a long rope over the closest one, and quickly knotted it into a crude hangman's noose, which he eased over Brogan's thick neck. A man about to commit suicide wouldn't bother with a neat knot, or so Steyn decided.

He fetched a high-backed wooden chair from the dining-room area nearby and placed it under the noose. Another snore came from behind him, but it was cut off halfway through.

Steyn spun round.

Brogan's eyes were open and he was staring blearily at the gunman.

"You!" he shouted in a thick voice, legs flailing as he attempted to rise. "What are you doing in my…"

"Cutting off loose ends, I'm afraid," Steyn replied calmly.

Then he yanked on the rope.

The noose tightened around Brogan's neck, lifting him to his feet. His shouts were abruptly cut off as he struggled and choked, eyes bulging.

Thickset and overweight, Brogan was heavier than Steyn, so Steyn looped the rope around the steel banister of the nearby stairway in order to anchor it. Then it was only necessary for him to pull with all his strength. Slowly but surely, the African manager's body was drawn into the air.

After knotting the rope around the banister and pushing over the dining-room chair, Steyn watched dispassionately as Brogan's kicks weakened. He was deciding what to write in the suicide note. Of course, the man was very drunk, as subsequent blood tests would eventually prove. That would certainly affect his coordination. A few words in a sprawling hand would be best: a rambling diatribe of how Brogan regretted what he had done, and couldn't live with the guilt of deceiving his boss, Dave, any longer.

Moving through the now-silent house, Steyn performed a quick search of Brogan's study, which yielded some company letterhead and a pen.

Sitting on the couch that Brogan had vacated just a few minutes earlier, Steyn bent to his task. He needed to hurry, because there was still one target to dispose of tonight…and he was going to take a deeply personal satisfaction in completing the final phase of his job.

CHAPTER 30

JOEY UNLOCKED HIS front door and walked tiredly inside. It was just after nine p.m., but now that his adrenaline had ebbed he felt as exhausted as if he'd pulled an all-nighter. But there was still an important job to do. He needed to look at Khosi's USB device and see what was stored on it. He thought he had a much better picture now of what it might, in fact, contain. Joey felt dread curl in his stomach as he plugged in his laptop and waited for it to power up.

He got a Coke from the fridge and took a gulp, feeling the sugar hit his bloodstream, providing a much-needed boost of energy. Sugar was a quick fix, even though you paid the price for it later, as Khosi had always joked.

Was that a noise coming from downstairs?

Joey put down the Coke can and listened, but the weird scraping sound he thought he'd heard was gone. All he could pick up was the soft humming of the laptop's fan.

Probably nothing. Even so, he should set the house alarm.

But when Joey tried to activate it, he found that the system was offline, the red buttons flashing randomly and the screen display blank.

That was strange. It had never happened before. Still, the storm had been violent, and a power surge might have damaged the control panel. He would have to sort it out in the morning.

Joey plugged Khosi's USB into the laptop, and felt the knots in his stomach tighten as he read the file headings.

"Initial Offer of Bribery to Stop Investigating Egoli East."

"My Investigation into Bribery—Who's Behind It?"

"Threats Against My Life."

"Information for Joey if Anything Happens."

Joey tensed as he heard another strange sound from below. What was it?

Tree branches, heavy with rain, scraping over the garage roof, perhaps?

Trying his best to ignore this distraction, Joey focused on his computer screen again.

CHAPTER 31

"WHAT DO YOU think of this hotel, baby girl? Quite something, isn't it?"

Isobel nodded in response to Dave's words, although she found she was too distracted, too shaken by everything she'd been through, to take in the sumptuous luxury of the Michelangelo Hotel in Sandton, where they had just arrived.

"I planned to bring you here later this year as a surprise. Thought we could have a second honeymoon. I wanted to book the presidential suite for us, but it wasn't available this time at such short notice, so we're in one of the premier king suites."

"It's lovely," Isobel tried bravely, even though she was trembling with exhaustion. "As long as it's safe, and there's a bed to sleep in."

Dave looked at her oddly. "Safe? Of course it's safe. Security here is top-notch, baby girl. Absolutely top."

Isobel couldn't help remembering the moment she had

gazed into the gunman's cold, pale eyes. He was out there, somewhere in this vast city.

Did he know where she was?

Isobel had done her best to keep a lookout for headlights behind them on the drive to Sandton. The journey had taken nearly an hour, and she was pretty sure that nobody had followed them all the way.

So, she might be safe enough in this hotel, and certainly security had seemed excellent, but what about Joey? She found her thoughts returning to him, and in a way that certainly wasn't appropriate right now. She remembered how the defined muscles in his forearms had tautened as he pulled the knotted rope tight, and how the crow's feet at the corners of his hazel eyes had crinkled up as he grinned at her.

She let out a frustrated sigh. Her recent encounter with Joey was blowing apart her resolution to be a better wife. She needed to have a serious talk with herself. It was time now to stop working at being an amateur sleuth and start working on her marriage.

"I organized for the boutique downstairs to send up a couple of garments," Dave said, and Isobel's eyes widened as she saw the selection of cocktail dresses hanging in the cupboard. "They're all your size. Wear the one you like the best and I'll buy it for you. If you want to take the others as well, no problem. There's a pair of shoes that should fit, too."

These were the dresses Dave liked her to wear—one silver, one turquoise, one black. Sleeveless, low-cut, body-hugging.

She had scratches on her shoulders that she'd acquired at some stage—probably while she was scrambling over the wall. She didn't really want to wear any of these gowns, and would have been happier going out in the jeans and long-sleeved top she'd bought from the chain store where they'd stopped to pick up cosmetics and underwear. But it wasn't her choice—not unless she wanted to risk the potential unpleasantness of an argument. She'd wear the jeans on the plane tomorrow. At least she'd be comfortable then.

She spent half an hour in the shower, washing away the dirt and grime and nervous sweat of the day. She made herself up, and put on the silver gown, because she thought Dave would probably like it the best.

She was putting on the high-heeled shoes when dread hit her like a fist in the stomach.

She had a gut feeling that Joey was in danger. She needed to call him, just to make sure that he was okay. Hearing his voice would set her mind at rest. She could reassure herself he was home safely, that his house alarm was turned on. She could thank him for saving her life…she just needed to find an excuse to have a moment alone with her phone.

She walked out of the bathroom, expecting Dave to compliment her on her appearance, but he was busy reading something on his computer and didn't even look up.

"I'm just going to…" she began, heading over to the table where her own phone lay, but at that moment the doorbell rang.

"Room service. I ordered us champagne," Dave said. "You want to get it, baby girl? I'm just finishing this report."

Well, perhaps Dave wouldn't notice if she headed outside for a minute. Grabbing her phone, she headed for the door.

But there was no champagne trolley waiting outside. Only a tall man, wearing black. His mouth quirked up in a weird, lopsided smile as he met her gaze. To her horror, Isobel recognized the cold, implacable eyes she was staring into.

CHAPTER 32

ISOBEL WAS TOO shocked to scream as she saw the dark barrel of the suppressor swing to aim at her. Her cell phone thudded down onto the carpet, dropping from fingers that were suddenly cold and nerveless.

There was a large laundry basket behind the tall man and she saw it was lined with thick, heavy-duty black plastic. He meant for her to go in there. That was how she was going to leave this place—bundled up in a tarp.

She felt as though she was moving in slow motion as she began to turn away, to run into the suite, to flee from him, even though she knew her efforts would be useless because his weapon was aimed at point-blank range.

And then she saw Dave, running to the door.

"Dave! Help!"

His hands were outstretched. He was going to fight Steyn off. Everything would be all right.

But Dave's left hand clapped hard over her mouth, cutting off her scream.

"Hold still," he hissed through gritted teeth. "Grab her, Steyn."

Out of the corner of her eye, she saw that Dave's right hand was holding a syringe filled with clear liquid.

Only then did Isobel realize the full extent of her betrayal.

Her husband was involved in this. Of course he was…how could he not have been? She only wished she'd realized this earlier. She had been too innocent, too trusting.

Now, there were two of them against her alone, but they meant to tranquilize her first, not shoot her. Perhaps that gave her a chance. She fought as wildly as she could, sinking her teeth into Dave's fingers so that he snatched his hand away with an angry shout. Before she could scream, Steyn's wiry hand clapped over her mouth in its place, crushing her lips. She tried to kick out at him but her ankle twisted in the ridiculous high heels and she stumbled back into her husband's grasp. Steyn's fingers moved to her throat, probing and pressing as his joker's smile widened. Black lights flashed in front of her eyes and she heard a weird, choking noise that she soon realized she was making.

Behind her, Dave was spluttering out words that made little sense to her, telling her that she was an interfering idiot woman, that they'd had everything sewn up so nicely until she'd come along and ripped it all apart, that this was her fault, she'd destroyed it all and she had only herself to blame for what happened next.

The syringe's silvery needle filled her vision. She felt the prick as it pierced her muscle. This was it…the end…the desperate violence of her struggles had not been enough. Two against one, it was never going to be.

Then, suddenly, it wasn't two against one anymore, because someone else had arrived.

Steyn was knocked off balance from behind, shoving Dave so that the needle ripped a bloody gouge on its way out of her skin. A shot rang out. Even with the suppressor it was surprisingly loud, and plaster rained from the ceiling. Dave let go of her arm and stumbled to his knees, and Isobel fell, sprawling onto the floor.

She looked up to see Joey, engaged in a silent, vicious fight with Steyn for ownership of his weapon.

Dave was up now, joining the melee so that it was two against one again. Well, there was something she could do about that. The syringe was still almost full, and it was lying within easy reach of her outstretched hand.

Isobel picked it up and stabbed it into her husband's right buttock before depressing the plunger as hard and fast as she could.

Dave turned, bellowing rage, and Isobel found herself fending off a windmill attack of blows that swiftly became weaker and less coordinated. She felt a surge of triumph…this was what he'd intended for her, and now he was suffering the effects. He slumped to the ground and she grabbed his hair and bashed his head down, grinding his face on the carpet, jamming a knee in his back as her silver skirt ripped to the thigh.

"It's okay," a voice panted from above her. "It's okay, Isobel. He's out for the count. Are you all right?"

Breathing hard, she stared up at Joey's concerned face. Was she all right? She hadn't been shot. Her throat was sore, her lips were tender, but she was still alive. Steyn lay unconscious on the ground, and Joey had fastened his hands tightly behind his back with a cable tie.

"How did you know?" Her head was whirling as Joey knelt down beside her. "How did you know about Dave?"

"My partner Khosi was investigating him before he died. Or before he was murdered, I should say. I spoke to the pathologist, who told me he was injected with a powerful tranquilizer normally used to sedate horses. I guess it was the same one they would have used on you. Then he was shot, to make it look like a suicide."

Isobel shivered as Joey continued.

"Before he died, Khosi saved everything on a USB device. They initially offered him a bribe to stop the investigation into Egoli East gold mine, and remove the security Private had placed there. He turned it down, and then decided to find out who was behind it. It was corruption at the highest level, Isobel. It went all the way to the government minister, Mr. Mashabela."

"How?" she asked, aware that her mouth was hanging open. Hastily, she closed it.

"Mr. Mashabela changed the laws to allow the illegal min-ing to operate and was getting kickbacks from Dave and Brogan. You thought Dave was losing money…in fact, he was making twenty times what he did with the transport business, and all tax free. They used the trucks to transport the illegal workers down from Zambia, and once those men were underground, they were basically prisoners, working until they were too weak to be productive. Then they'd be shuttled back and another team would be sourced from another village."

"Human trafficking. My husband is a human trafficker." Isobel's voice shook. His involvement in illegal gold mining had been shocking enough, but this crime was more horrific than anything she could have imagined.

"Not anymore," Joey told her in a firm voice, but she had no idea whether he meant Dave wouldn't be trafficking anymore, or would no longer be her husband. Both appealed. Joey stood up and held out a hand.

Isobel kicked off her ridiculous shoes before taking his hand. She still felt dizzy, and she didn't know if she should start laughing, or throw up, or kiss him. Probably only one of the three was advisable, and as he helped her to her feet and she wrapped her arms around him, Isobel started to get a pretty good idea which one it was going to be.

EPILOGUE

Six months later

ISOBEL WAS FEELING surprisingly nervous. It was the official opening of the new headquarters of Private Johannesburg, in a penthouse office suite in the Sandton CBD. She and Joey had gone into partnership together after the arrest of the illegal mining kingpins, including her ex-husband Dave and the government minister Mr. Mashabela.

Steyn was arrested, but committed suicide in prison soon afterward. One of the warders told her that he'd written GET ME OUT OF THIS TRAP in his own blood on the wall before he had died.

Somehow, she thought that was poetic justice.

Isobel wasn't nervous about the firm, although she'd initially had misgivings about venturing into a partnership with her new boyfriend, who'd since become her fiancé. But as it turned out, they were as happy together during working hours as they were outside of them, and in fact, they made a damned good team. The business had taken off and they were now extremely busy.

So Isobel wasn't worried about that.

But she was very nervous about meeting the new intern, just turned sixteen years old, who had volunteered to help out during her school holidays.

Isobel glanced in the mirror as she passed the reception desk. Her blond hair was in place, her white top and blue jeans neat, no embarrassing coffee stains or lipstick smudges or anything a teenager would pick up on. Well, then. No reason to delay this moment any longer.

"Hi, Hayley," she said, approaching the cubicle where the young woman was already hard at work. Isobel saw that her desk was spotless, and a poster of Metallica had already been put up on the wall.

The teenager turned. She was an attractive girl and Isobel could instantly see the resemblance to her father. But when she stood up, grinning from ear to ear, and gave Isobel a big, warm hug—only then did Isobel really believe that everything would be okay.

ABOUT THE AUTHORS

James Patterson has written more bestsellers and created more enduring fictional characters than any other novelist writing today. He lives in Florida with his family.

Jassy Mackenzie is the author of the Jade de Jong series. She lives in South Africa.

DR. CROSS, THE SUSPECT IS YOUR PATIENT.

An anonymous caller has promised to set off deadly bombs in Washington, DC. A cruel hoax or the real deal? By the time Alex Cross and his wife, Bree Stone, uncover the chilling truth, it may already be too late....

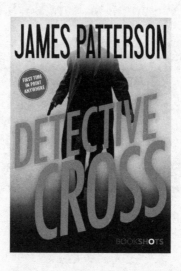

Read the thrilling new addition to the Alex Cross series,
Detective Cross, **available only from**

BOOK**SHOTS**

Also check out:
Cross Kill

 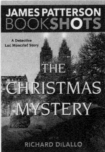 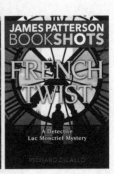

"DID MY BROTHER KILL YOUR HUSBAND?"
MITCHUM IS BACK.

His brother's been charged with murder. Nathaniel swears he
didn't kill anyone, but he was sleeping with the victim's wife.
Now, Navy SEAL dropout Mitchum will break every rule to
expose the truth—even if it destroys the people he loves.

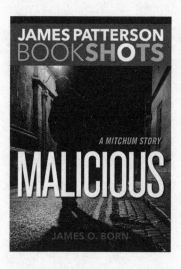

Read the thrilling sequel to *Hidden*:
Malicious

Available only from

BOOK**SHOTS**

HE'S WORTH MILLIONS...
BUT HE'S WORTHLESS WITHOUT HER.

Siobhan Dempsey came to New York with a purpose: she wants to become a successful artist. But then she meets tech billionaire Derick Miller, who takes her breath away. And though Siobhan's body comes alive at his touch, their relationship has been a roller-coaster ride.

Are they meant to be together?

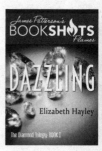  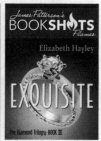

Read the steamy Diamond Trilogy books:

Dazzling, The Diamond Trilogy: Book I

Radiant, The Diamond Trilogy: Book II

Exquisite, The Diamond Trilogy: Book III

Available only from

W